The first kiss

Slowly, deliberately, Carlos took Marina in his arms. She felt the first touch of his mouth, gentle yet insistent. She had never been kissed like this before . . . then the kiss that started so softly became harder, hungrier, and more possessive.

This was ecstasy, a thrill, a joy she had never experienced in her whole life. She felt she couldn't breathe, and yet breath was unnecessary; she was floating upward into a realm of glory beyond anything she had ever known. Only when Carlos took his lips from hers did she realize that she was trembling.

Suddenly he moved away from her. "I shouldn't have done that," he said, his voice empty, almost weary. "I'm leaving tomorrow."

And Marina knew that he would not, could not, take her with him. . . .

Also in Pyramid Books

by

BARBARA CARTLAND

LOVE ON THE RUN

Barbara Cartland

PYRAMID BOOKS
NEW YORK

LOVE ON THE RUN

A PYRAMID BOOK

Pyramid edition published July 1973

©Barbara McCorquodale 1965

©Barbara Cartland 1969

All Rights Reserved

ISBN 0–515–03079–1

Printed in the United States of America

Pyramid Books are published by Pyramid Communications, Inc.
Its trademarks, consisting of the word "Pyramid" and the
portrayal of a pyramid, are registered in the United States
Patent Office.

Pyramid Communications, Inc., 919 Third Avenue, New York,
New York 10022

1

"It can't be true!"

Victor's voice sounded incredulous. Marina turned from the window.

"I'm sorry, Victor," she said, "terribly sorry."

"What the hell do you mean, you're sorry?" he asked.

She made a helpless gesture with her hands.

"Just one of those things," she answered. "I've tried; honestly I've tried, Victor, to think it would all work out; but it's no use. I just can't go on acting a lie. I don't love you. It's no use pretending I do."

"It's much too soon for you to be sure," he protested. "Give it a proper trial. Come away with me on a holiday and take the yacht—a few close friends and we can be together. Come to that, we needn't even take the friends."

Marina turned back to the window.

"It's no use," she said wearily. "I've thought and thought; I've lain awake at night going over it. We're just not right for each other."

Victor Harrison moved across the room and lit a cigarette. He shut the lighter with a crack which sounded angry, and set it down with a bang on the polished table.

Marina turned to look at him. The expression in her eyes was gentle. She knew that in a way she was hitting below the belt. It was not only losing her . . . there was so much more to it than that.

Women never turned Victor Harrison down. He was rich and powerful enough to get everything he wanted; almost everything, anyway. That life had been unusually generous to him in the past wasn't going to make this knock any easier to take.

She saw the set of his jaw, the hard line of his lips and thought, with a sudden little pang, she very nearly loved him.

It ought to be easy to love Victor. He was a very nice person. A man not particularly spoilt by the fact that he was an enormous social success, a friend of the younger Royals, an intimate of the President of the United States, the social lion wherever he went, whether it was Paris, New York, Hongkong or Buenos Aires.

He was one of those people who made friends everywhere because he was obviously so friendly. It was not only his great wealth that attracted them. It was Victor himself. And Marina had to admit to herself that when she first met him she had been attracted by the man.

"Is there anyone else?" she heard his voice, harsh with an undertone of pain, ask the conventional question.

"No, of course there isn't," Marina replied. "If there were I would tell you."

"Then where have we failed?"

There was a slight hesitation before the pronoun. Marina knew that Victor could not bear to take all the blame.

"We haven't," she said, moving towards him till they stood facing each other in front of the beautiful marble Adam fireplace. "It's my fault entirely. I ought never to have consented to an engagement. You see, I knew from the very beginning that I didn't really love you."

He threw his cigarette almost savagely into the fireplace.

"Love! Love!" he ejaculated. "You expect too much, Marina. I love you, I adore you. I can teach you what love means after we are married. You can't expect it to be all the rapture you read about in books."

"I think that is what I do expect," Marina said almost beneath her breath.

"But how do you know it's possible for you to feel that way?" Victor asked. "Some girls are not so emotionally aroused as others. Surely you must understand that. What chance do we really get, you and I? We are never alone together, but always surrounded by people, parties, crowds—the herd!"

He moved towards her and took her hand in his.

"Come away with me, Marina. Let's go somewhere where we can really be alone—Tahiti perhaps—the West Indies—anywhere we can bathe, talk and really sort things out together."

His voice was pleading. For a moment Marina seemed to hesitate before she slowly shook her head.

"Damn you, you are being obstinate," Victor said.

His arms were round her shoulders. He was drawing her closer to him.

"Marina, listen to me. You haven't given it a proper trial. I know we are right for each other. In fact I know you are the only woman in the world for me. I love you as I have never loved anyone else before. Let me teach you to love me too."

His voice dropped almost to a whisper. Now his lips were seeking hers, hungrily, possessively.

She made no effort to elude him. She just stood motionless within his arms. He kissed her wildly, passionately, with an intensity which was spurred on by his fear of losing her.

7

"I love you, I love you," he murmured over and over again, as his mouth bruised her and his arms held her like a vice.

She was so tiny and slender, her head coming only to his shoulder, that he seemed almost to overpower her, and yet she made no effort to escape. Her mouth was soft beneath his, but there was no response, no flicker of life, no fire to equal his own—only a softness which was not at all the answer to his demands.

She felt his passion rage over her; then suddenly, as if her indifference to his kisses reached his consciousness, he let her go. He stood staring down at her, breathing quickly, his eyes dark with passion; his hands which had held her so tightly, clenched at his sides.

"Blast you!" he said. The words seemed to be jerked from him. "It means nothing to you, does it?"

The very roughness of his tone told her how much he was suffering.

"Oh, darling Victor, forgive me!" Marina said, and her hands went out towards him.

He moved away from her.

"Leave me alone," he said gruffly.

He walked across the room to a side table and helped himself to a large whisky and soda. Marina knew he was struggling for self-control. She watched him with compassionate eyes.

He drank off the whisky and set the glass down on the table and turned towards the door.

"Victor, where are you going?" The question was startled from between her lips. For a moment there was the hint of a smile on his drawn face.

"I suppose the conventional answer is 'To the Devil,'" he replied.

"But Victor . . ." Marina began, only to be silenced when he interrupted her.

"It's all right, Sweetie, I'm not going to blow my brains out or anything like that. I'm just going to lick my wounds and then start the assault over again. I don't give in easily, you know that."

Marina moved her lips to reply. It was too late. He had opened the door, passed through it, slammed it decisively behind him before she could articulate a word.

For a moment she stood staring at the closed door, and then she sat down on the sofa and put her hands up to her face. It had been worse, much worse than she had anticipated.

She had lain awake all night wondering how she could tell him, how she could admit having made a mistake in the first place in saying that they could be engaged. Thank goodness it had not been officially announced—the Press would have headlined the break! But all their closest friends knew.

She was well aware that Victor would come in for a lot of sympathy from those who had always thought her spoiled or were jealous both of her money and of her success with men.

"At least, no one can say I am marrying you for your money," Victor said once, and she had laughed and agreed that nothing could be more suitable than that two really rich people should marry each other.

Sometimes she had wondered if that had not been half the trouble. They had nothing, really, to give to each other—cufflinks from Cartier which were equalled by charm bracelets from Boucheron. There was not the same thrill, she thought whimsically, when one knew one could buy the present oneself without noticing the expenditure.

"Oh, what's wrong with me? What do I want?" she had asked in the darkness during the night. Now she said it again.

She looked round the huge, comfortable Mayfair flat which had been her home for the last three months; in fact, ever since she had been engaged to Victor. It was a magnificent flat and cost almost a king's ransom to rent. It was not hers; it was just something she was able to acquire temporarily because she could afford it.

She thought now that was one of the reasons why she had wanted to be married, so that she could have a place of her very own.

Her Trustees had always refused to let her acquire a house in London or New York, or even, as she had once dreamed, a château near Paris. They pointed out that it would add to her obligations; but she had known the real answer was that they expected her to get married, and thought perhaps her husband would have a house, or houses, and then hers would be superfluous.

It was a reasonable idea. Marina admitted that. What made it so difficult was that those who dealt with her great wealth or with her personal affairs were invariably so reasonable and so right.

She rose from the sofa and as she did so she caught a glimpse of herself in the long gilt-framed mirror which hung on the wall. Naturally she was expected to marry. Who else in the world had such great wealth and combined with it so much beauty?

She was slim with an exquisite figure and her golden hair with a touch of red in it owed nothing to the hairdresser's art. Her eyes, which were surprisingly almost purple, were fringed with natural, dark lashes and her heart-shaped face sent portrait painters wild with delight.

Marina looked at her reflection and sighed.

"Perhaps I have everything but a heart," she said aloud to herself; but she knew it was untrue.

10

Once, many years ago, shortly before she had left school, she had felt the first tremulous awakening of love. It had only been the ridiculous passion of a school-girl for a man much older than herself who treated her as a child and married someone else.

Afterwards, when the first agony was over, she had looked back and realised there was no one to blame, and it was not in the least his fault because he did not realise that she was growing up. But the ecstatic joy of her feelings unfolded within her, the sudden leaping as of a tiny flame, had remained with her as a mocking memory.

Yet by comparison all the emotions she had felt since for other men paled into insignificance. She knew what she was seeking.

It was that love which she had once known for all too brief a moment—a love so beautiful, so wonderful, so entirely and completely divine that she knew she must spend her whole life looking for it again.

She had given in to Victor's insistence because she was lonely. How people would laugh, she thought, if they knew the truth. The fabulous Marina Martyn admitting she was lonely amid the social whirl of not one country, but of half a dozen which treated her as an honoured and privileged guest.

Her father had been English, and her mother was a member of one of the oldest and most distinguished of Virginian families. Her grandmother had been French, and yet another grandmother, far back in her father's ancestry, had been Italian. She had relations all over the world who loved and welcomed Marina whenever she appeared among them—and yet she was lonely.

"I have never had a real home of my own," she had confided to Victor when he asked her to marry him.

"I will give you a dozen," he had answered and she had known as he said it, it was not the reply she wanted.

Her father had died when she was five. Her mother had married again a man whom Marina detested; and then, three years later, she had broken her neck while out hunting.

After that there had been a series of kind aunts and uncles, cousins and old friends who had been only too willing to have the privilege of looking after her. And as she had grown older, there had been Trustees and secretaries, lady's maids and chauffeurs— a whole retinue of people to wait on her, to pander to her every whim.

Yet no one had ever filled the empty place within her heart or dulled the aching want of which she was so often conscious and which she tried to tell herself scornfully was merely a psychological reaction to being an orphan.

What a fool she had been to think that Victor could give her all the things she had never had, which no money, not even her own millions, could buy! Poor Victor! The very words set him into a different category from that in which he had been before.

Then she remembered his drawn face turned towards her, and his voice, firm and resolute saying, "I will return to start the assault all over again."

With almost a cry Marina turned and went from the room. She crossed the hall and opened the door of another room where three secretaries were working at desks piled with correspondence and loaded with telephones.

"Sybil," she said to an attractive girl of about twenty-five who had just set down one of the telephones as she entered.

"Yes, Miss Martyn?"

12

"I want you a moment."

Marina walked back into the hall, and passing down a long corridor went into her bedroom. It was a huge room overlooking Grosvenor Square. The leaves on the trees in the Square were the soft, pale green of spring and the crocuses were out round the statue of President Roosevelt.

Marina crossed over the soft blue carpet, which was like the sky outside, and sat down at her dressing-table with its big triple mirror. She moved almost automatically as if she was thinking of something else, and only when she heard Sybil O'Connell shut the door behind her did she turn round on the stool to face her chief secretary.

"What is it, Miss Martyn?" Sybil enquired, startled at the pallor of her employer's face.

"Sybil, I've got to get away," Marina replied.

"Away?" Sybil O'Connell asked in her soft Irish voice. Marina nodded.

"But everyone is expecting you to stay here for the season," Sybil said; "you know that is what was planned."

"You don't understand," Marina said. "I've broken off my engagement, Sybil."

"Oh, no!" Sybil was genuinely startled. "Mr. Harrison is so nice. I thought you were so happy. We were all so pleased about it."

"I don't love him," Marina said. "There is no other reason, Sybil. He is nice. He is everything you all think him. But I don't love him."

Sybil O'Connell hesitated.

"You don't think . . .?"

Marina, sitting on the stool, looked up at her.

"Look at me, Sybil," she said. "We've known each other a long time. You have worked for me for five years, isn't that right?"

Sybil nodded.

"Then tell me honestly," Marina went on, "tell me on your oath, do you really believe that people fall in love just because someone else loves them? Do you really think I shall grow to love Victor, not loving him now?"

For a moment Sybil O'Connell did not answer. Then her eyes flickered; she looked away from the questioning gaze of her employer.

"I wouldn't like to answer that question, Miss Martyn," she said.

"Yes you would, and you've got to," Marina insisted. "Nobody knows me better than you. You know Victor too. Tell me the honest truth, Sybil. Because I know you are a religious person, it has got to be the truth. Will I ever fall in love with him?"

"There is of course a chance . . ."

Marina gave a little sigh.

"You've answered me, Sybil. The answer is 'No'. There is always the thousandth chance in everything: the miracle, if you like, but I don't believe in miracles where Victor and I are concerned."

"It seems such a pity," Sybil O'Connell said.

"Why?" Marina asked. "Because we are both so rich, because people can go round saying, 'At least they are not marrying each other for what they can get out of it?' That isn't going to make a marriage. That isn't the right foundation on which to build a home and family. There must be other things . . . there must be."

The tone of her voice caught at Sybil's heartstrings.

"You poor child," she said, forgetting for a moment that she had always been slightly frightened of her employer. "It must have been hard to tell him."

"It was," Marina said, "and that is why I have to

go away. You do see, Sybil. He has to get over it. I have to get over it too. I can't see him every day; I can't have him pleading with me. I can't go on saying 'No'. I couldn't stand it."

"Then where shall we go?" Sybil O'Connell said in a practical manner.

"There is no 'we'," Marina answered. "I'm going alone."

She saw with surprise the protest in Sybil's face.

"Don't be stupid!" she went on. "He would follow us, you know he would; and how can Marina Martyn with her usual royal retinue hide herself? As I step out of the 'plane, the Public Relations Officer will be waiting. When I arrive at the hotel, the newspaper reporters will be in the hall. No, Sybil, think of something better. I want to go alone."

"But of course you can't do that," Sybil O'Connell said.

"Why not?" Marina flashed. "I'm twenty-one. I suppose I'm the most travelled girl in the whole world. The only thing is, I've never gone anywhere alone, by myself. I've always had the 'court circle' to protect me and imprison me."

"We tried not to do that," Sybil expostulated.

"Sybil, you've always been an angel," Marina exclaimed. "But you have your hours off, your time when you can get away, when you can just be yourself without people staring and looking at you and asking questions, wondering whether you are hot or cold, trying almost too hard to make you happy! Just for once, I've got to get to know myself."

"I never imagined you could feel like that," Sybil O'Connell said, "but I do understand."

"I thought you would: so will you help me? Where shall I go?"

"Wherever you go, people will recognise you," Sybil said.

"Will they?" Marina questioned. "They will recognise Marina Martyn, of course, if she arrives at an hotel with the rooms booked, a fleet of cars to meet her at the station; red carpet down; the best suite filled with flowers. Oh, you know the whole routine! But supposing quite an ordinary girl arrives alone, even they would not imagine for one moment that she is Marina Martyn."

"I suppose it would depend on where you went," Sybil answered. "In Paris, for instance, you seem to know every other person. One might say the same for Rome or Venice or New York—or even Cannes for that matter."

"I know! I know!" Marina interrupted. "That's why I am asking you—'Where shall I go?'"

Sybil put her fingers to her temples.

"Am I really hearing this conversation?" she asked. "It doesn't seem real, somehow."

"It is, all the same," Marina said. "I want to get away. I've got to get away and I'm going to get away. Quite frankly, no one is going to stop me."

"Oughtn't we to tell your Trustees or someone?"

"Who?" Marina asked. "When it comes down to things, Sybil, who really cares? My Trustees don't. Since Uncle George died, the majority of them are too elderly to take any interest except Cousin Richard; and he, if I remember rightly, when we last heard from him was big-game shooting in Africa; so it's going to be some time before you can get in touch with him."

"It's frightening, if you think about it," Sybil said.

"Of course, it's like pulling the bung out of the bottom of the boat!" Marina replied. "Nothing seems secure; nothing seems so solid as it did a few moments

16

ago, just because I've asked for what the majority of sensible people want occasionally—to be alone."

"You sound like Greta Garbo," Sybil said accusingly.

"I know what she must have felt," Marina replied. "I want to go away: I want to think, but most of all I want to avoid Victor. Now let's come back to the original question. Where can I go?"

"It'll have to be somewhere in Europe," Sybil answered. "I can't bear you to go further: it would be too frightening, too much of a responsibility for me."

Marina shrugged her shoulders.

"Very well—Europe," she agreed. "It doesn't really matter. As you see, I'm not particular."

"It can't be Spain. You were there last year," Sybil said reflectively. "The papers had your picture on every page. France is impossible and so, of course, is Italy. You don't like Germany; you were in Copenhagen last Easter. Oh Heavens! There doesn't seem to be anywhere!"

"What about Portugal?" Marina asked. "As it happens I've never been there."

"Nor you have," Sybil agreed. "It's a good idea! Shall I try and book you . . ."

"Stop!" Marina interrupted. "That's one thing you mustn't do, don't you see? I've just got to go off into the blue and you're to be the only person who knows where I've gone. You've got to swear to me on the Bible that you'll tell no one—no one at all."

"Well, I suppose you'll go to Lisbon," Sybil said in the tone of one who accepts the inevitable with a kind of philosophic calmness.

"No, I shall not go to Lisbon. It's a town," Marina said "and I hate towns. I've had too much of them. What's that place near Lisbon? The place where ex-kings and queens all retire to. I seem to have read a lot about it."

"Estoril," Sybil told her.

"Yes, that's it. That's where I'll go. There must be a decent hotel there: in fact, I expect there are several."

"How long do you think you'll go for?"

"I don't know," Marina answered. "That makes it somewhat of an adventure. I don't know how long I'm going for, nor what I'll do when I get there. You see, I've never been alone before. That'll be an excitement in itself."

"You may find it terribly dull," Sybil warned.

"In which case, I shall come home. I was never one to like suffering for suffering's sake."

"Let me at least telephone to see if I can get you some nice rooms."

"You'll do nothing of the sort," Marina said. "I'm going to do all that myself, when I get there. And, by the way, I shall want another name and another passport."

Sybil looked at her in astonishment.

"But that's impossible!"

"Of course it isn't. People are always having false passports in books. It must be possible to get hold of one."

"I'm sure it isn't—at least we don't know how to do such a thing."

"Then what's the point of my going away?" Marina asked angrily. "Even in Portugal, people will undoubtedly have heard of Marina Martyn and in two minutes the whole commotion will start, and I shan't even have you there to protect me."

"Don't go then," Sybil said coaxingly.

"If I don't get away, I think I shall go mad," Marina said a little drearily. "That is an exaggeration, of course. Don't you understand? I can't face Victor. I like him too much not to feel sorry for him and very ashamed of myself. I just couldn't stand scene after scene; argument after argument. Victor is the persistent kind. You know that as well as I do. He is not going to give up very easily."

"He has left the flat," Sybil said hesitantly. "Where do you think he has gone now?"

"If you offered me three guesses, I should say he had gone to Cartier to buy me the most expensive bracelet he could fine, and he will no doubt arrive at dinner time with a huge bouquet of orchids having convinced himself that the whole thing was a lovers' quarrel which can be made up with a few kisses and a box of chocolates."

"That sounds cynical," Sybil said accusingly.

"I am not: I am desperate," Marina answered.

Sybil seemed to be thinking for a moment and then she said suddenly:

"I've got an idea! You remember Mary Marshall?"

"Mary Marshall? . . . Mary Marshall?" Marina repeated, "the name seems familiar. Who is she?"

"A girl we took on a fortnight ago in the Accounts Department."

Marina nodded. There was a big office in the City where her affairs were handled by a number of extremely efficient accountants who saw to her investments, who dealt with her Income Tax and who generally smoothed the golden path on which she had walked ever since her father died.

Occasionally, when she was in London, Marina called in as a duty to thank those who worked for her for their services; and she remembered now that one of her friends had asked her to get a relation a job.

Mary Marshall had been living in Australia, but was desperately anxious to come to England. It had been the dream of her life, and it had been so easy for Marina to tell Sybil to arrange it.

The girl had called at the flat to thank her benefactor. Marina, who was giving a cocktail party at the time, had asked her in, introduced her to her friends and given her a glass of sherry. It had all been as easy as that. And she had forgotten all about her until this moment.

"Yes, I remember Mary Marshall," she told Sybil. "What has she got to do with it?"

"She had to have her passport renewed," Sybil answered, "and it was sent here with a form for you to sign because you are her employer. I signed it for you, as I always do. The passport is in my office. It suddenly struck me that you are not unlike her."

Marina's eyes widened.

"Get it, Sybil. Get it quickly!" she cried.

Sybil O'Connell went out of the room and Marina picked up the house telephone which was standing on the small inlaid gilt table. She pressed the button which communicated with her maid's bedroom.

"Is that Annie?" she asked. "I'm going away for a few days. Will you pack some plain, light clothes? Yes . . . jersey suits and two or three very simple cocktail dresses . . . Nothing elaborate . . . low-heeled sandals . . . I think I may be going to the sea. No, no jewellery. As quickly as possible, please."

As she replaced the receiver Sybil came into the room carrying the passport. The passport photograph had been badly taken by a cheap photographer. It might have been any girl—a small, heart-shaped face and large, dark eyes.

"A good thing it isn't in colour," Sybil said. "Mary Marshall has almost ash blonde hair."

"It quite easily could be me," Marina said, almost in surprise.

20

"What really made me think of it was the initials are the same," Sybil told her. "After all, nearly everything you have has M.M. scrawled over it."

"You would have made a good detective," Marina said. "I've told Annie to pack my things. There is one thing you might do for me. Ring up and see if I can catch an afternoon aeroplane to Lisbon. Don't give my name."

She paused and laughed.

"I had forgotten. Of course I want a seat for Miss Marshall!"

"I don't think we really ought to do this," Sybil said in a flurry. "I am sure there is some ghastly penalty attached to using someone else's passport."

"I won't let you go to prison," Marina said. "I will say I coerced you into doing whatever you are doing for me. I'm sure Mary Marshall won't want her passport in the meantime."

"If she does, I'll say I haven't had it back from the Passport Office," Sybil said.

"You are getting quite into the spirit of the adventure," Marina smiled approvingly.

"You must take your own passport, too," Sybil said positively. "You may get into trouble and then at least you can identify yourself."

"You think of everything," Marina told her.

"Will you promise me one thing?" Sybil went on. "Will you telephone when you arrive and let me know your address? Supposing anything happened?"

"What sort of thing?" Marina asked.

"Fire . . . burglary . . . someone dying."

Marina looked at her.

"You see," she said, "how really unimportant I am in all the things that matter. If it was anyone else, you would say 'Your mother might be ill' or 'Your father might be involved in an accident.' 'Your sister might have a baby' or 'Your brother got a new job.' None of those things applies to me. If the flat burns down, it isn't mine. The only thing you can't burn is all the money which has always stood like a plate-glass window between me and the world."

"Miss Martyn, that's ungrateful" Sybil said. "After all, most people would give their right hands to be in your shoes."

"Most people are silly fools," Marina answered, "and well you know it!"

She gave a little laugh.

"Oh, Sybil, I feel quite gay! Don't try and spoil everything the first time in my life I've had the courage to run away from my nursemaids!"

"I thought we were making you happy," Sybil said sadly.

Marina bent forward and kissed her on the cheek.

"You are a dear and I am terribly fond of you but just for once I'm going to be me. If I get into any real difficulties, I'll send for you to get me out of them."

"You promise?" Sybil said, suddenly serious.

"What could happen to me except that I might run out of money?"

"Heavens! I had almost forgotten!" Sybil cried.

She ran out of the room and Marina gave a little smile at her retreating back. She was fond of Sybil but she was indeed very like a fussy nursemaid always worrying in case one of the intricate arrangements should go wrong—a car that was ordered would not turn up, or an aeroplane not start to time. Victor or no Victor it would be fun to let things go their own way and not become almost hysterical if things were not so smooth as they should be.

An hour later Marina slipped down the back stairs

of the flats and out into a mews. She had refused to use either the lifts or the front entrance.

"The porters will see that I am leaving and think it very strange," she said to Sybil who was almost shocked at Marina's idea of such stealth and subterfuge.

"You know perfectly well," she told Sybil, "that if Victor thought I had left the country, he would bribe the porter to tell him I had gone to London Airport, and he would pester the people at the Airport to say where I've gone. He is going to be very angry when he finds that the bird in the gilded cage has flown away."

"He'll know when you come back?" Sybil asked.

"Yes, of course," Marina answered. "But at least it will give us both time to get over the initial shock."

The two girls found a taxi and Sybil, who was carrying Marina's case put it inside.

"Are you quite sure you've got enough money?" she asked in an anxious whisper.

"If I haven't, I'll wire you to send me some," Marina answered.

"You'll let me know where you are staying?"

"I'll think about it," Marina answered. "Good-bye Sybil, you've been an angel."

She slammed the door and told the man through the inside window to go to London Airport.

"It's a long way," he grumbled. "I don't know if I've got enough petrol for that."

"I'll give you a pound over the fare," Marina answered and then remembered that that in itself was very out of keeping with her new personality.

Mary Marshall would doubtless have been very careful with her money. In which case, she thought, she would have taken the 'bus from the Air Terminal.

"I think we'll allow Mary Marshall to be a little richer than the average typist taking a holiday," Marina told herself. Then she gave a little shrug and sat back comfortably in the taxi.

She felt suddenly free. She felt as though she had left her worries and unhappiness behind and shifted a huge burden from her shoulders. She remembered that it was the first time in her life she had ever gone to London Airport in a taxi.

Before, there had always been large, smooth-running cars to carry her there. It was the first time that there hadn't been someone to travel with her, to handle her ticket, to see that the Station Officer or the Airline representative ushered her safely into the right aeroplane.

"I'm alone," Marina told herself, and found she'd said it aloud, and the surprise in her voice was very obvious, even to her own ears. "I'm alone."

The noise of the traffic seemed to grind out the words over and over again. She thought of Victor coming back that evening, as she had predicted, with the orchids and the present from Cartier. She had an idea he would bring her a diamond bracelet. Victor always expected women to like diamond bracelets. In fact, he had never found a woman who didn't.

She wondered what Sybil would say to him. Poor Sybil, who would have to stand up to face his incredulity and then his anger.

Victor was not an easy person to handle; but Sybil, whatever pressure he might use, would be loyal. Marina knew that. She thought how lucky she was to have Sybil not only as an employee but as a friend.

It was almost the first time that she had felt grateful·for her. It was a new sensation and she felt a little ashamed that she had not realised before how much the older girl meant to her.

"I suppose I'm spoilt," Marina thought to herself. "Perhaps as Mary Marshall I shall find a new me: someone much nicer, much kinder and even more interesting."

Then she realised that it was not for a new self she was looking; it was not really that she was escaping from Victor, it was what she wanted to sort out in her own mind.

She wanted to be quite certain of the thing that she had been searching for all her life—Love, that strong, demanding, unforgettable love which, although she hardly dared admit it to herself, had always haunted her dreams.

2

Marina awoke and wondered where she was!

Then, as the outlines of the hotel bedroom became clear in the sunlight seeping through the curtains, she remembered that she was alone in a strange country.

For a moment she felt a little pang of dismay. It was almost one of nostalgia for the familiar things— her maid coming softly into the room to draw her curtains and bring her breakfast; Sybil and the other secretaries waiting downstairs; the buzz of the house telephone; the chauffeur with her own car, ready to take her wherever she might wish to go.

And above all, Victor ringing her on the telephone, as he had done every morning these past months, to tell her he loved her, so that she would start the day in the warm glow of being attractive and wanted! And what woman should ask for more?

Last night, in the darkness she had felt depressed. The first elation of running away from everything she knew, and from Victor, had passed quickly. But the time the aeroplane had crossed the Channel she was beginning to regret her impetuous haste, and when finally they touched down at Lisbon Airport, she had to fight against an almost uncontrollable impulse to take the next aeroplane home.

It had all been strange and unfamiliar. The struggle to collect her luggage and get it through the Customs and on to a taxi had been something she had never had to do before.

To arrive at the hotel and encounter the polite indifference which the Reception accorded to Mary Marshall was very different from the excited obsequiousness which was invariably accorded Marina Martyn.

She had picked her hotel at random from a Guide to Portugal that she had found aboard the aeroplane. It was obviously the best and she had been glad to see that the luxury and the comfort in the lounge and along the corridors were of the type to which she had been accustomed.

The bedroom, however, was certainly not the Royal suite and she had taken it without comment because she had not wished to draw attention to herself. It was comfortable enough with one window looking out towards the sea, and the other towards a clump of trees which protected the front door of the hotel, and through which she could see modern villas with their flat roofs and gaily painted shutters.

All this had been perceptible at night by the floodlighting which illuminated the hotel, and yet the surroundings had not been able to dispel the cloud of depression which had made Marina creep into bed and in the darkness shed a few tears into her pillow.

It was years since she had cried. She was really not certain what she was crying about—perhaps her lost dreams of happiness with Victor. Why couldn't she love him?

She woke in the night and asked herself the question over and over again and could find no answer. He was in fact a lovable person and certainly not more spoilt than any of the other rich young men she knew.

27

"I wanted to love him," she sobbed drearily. "I wanted us to be happy together."

Now she had landed herself in a rather ridiculous situation: she had run away from all her comforts and friends just because she couldn't face up to Victor's insistence.

With an effort Marina threw back the bedclothes and jumped out of bed. What was the point of lying there thinking about it. She must have been awake half the night. She remembered seeing the first faint fingers of light at the sides of the window before finally she fell asleep.

Her eyes felt heavy and she knew that when she looked at herself in the mirror there would be traces of her tears. Then, as she flung back the curtains, the sun flooded in brilliant and dazzling, and the sea was vividly blue with white waves breaking on the shore.

Her spirit surged upwards. This was very different from the pale, rain-washed skies of spring in England. There was a bougainvillaea growing on the wall below, startling purple against some scarlet geraniums; and the houses with their painted shutters, which she had noticed the night before, were a kaleidoscope of colour as though an artist had gone through the whole range of his palette.

Marina leaned her elbows on the window sill and stood staring out.

Below her was a donkey wearing a hat, its long ears peeping ridiculously through the straw corn, and on its legs it wore short white pantaloons to protect it from the flies. The cart it was pulling was massed high with flowers—lilies, irises and carnations—and the woman selling them, with her black hair and thick black gown, looked like someone out of an ancient print.

"It's spring, I'm young and this is an adventure!" Marina said the words aloud and when she turned from the window she was smiling and her eyes were sparkling.

She rang the bell and ordered breakfast from a solemn-faced young German, who she guessed was in the country to learn the language, before she went into the bathroom to draw her own bath.

An hour later she walked out of the hotel, wearing a vivid pink jersey suit which she felt was somehow appropriate to the festival of colour she saw all around her.

She walked down the small promenade which bordered the golden beach. There were a few holiday-makers; but it was still early in the season. She had the feeling of having the world to herself.

She walked for some way and then sat down to watch the scene around her. What was she going to do with herself?

It was funny to feel that nothing was planned; nothing was organised for the hours that lay ahead. There was no Sybil waiting with a long list of things she had to do, or things that might amuse her. If she did do anything, she would have to find it out for herself.

The thought of Sybil made her remember that just as she had been leaving the flat and her suitcase was finally packed, Sybil had thrust a book into her hands and with it a piece of paper.

"I haven't had time to look up much," she said. "The book will tell you a little about the history of Portugal, and I have written down some of the restaurants which Jean tells me are amusing. Apparently she spent part of her holiday in Portugal last year."

Jean was an elderly secretary who took life extremely seriously and Marina did not feel that

Jean's experiences would be much help. Yet, now remembering what Sybil had said, she opened her handbag and searched among her note-case and her passport for the piece of paper that Sybil had given her.

She opened it carefully against the wind blowing from the sea and threatening to blow it out of her hand. It was a list of places of historical interest—the Madre de Dios, a church which Jean thought was the most beautiful she had ever seen, and then a few hints on restaurants.

Solmar, the first written in Jean's careful hand was where apparently one could choose delicious fish from the aquarium in the restaurant, the second was *Furnas Langosteiras* against which she had put 'A Café along the coast where one can choose lobsters and crabs from the caves into which they are washed by the sea. Interesting and unusual.'

Marina made a little face as if she thought it wouldn't prove particularly amusing; but nevertheless obediently, because there was nothing else to do, she put the paper away in her handbag and looked around for a taxi.

She found one so small that she almost had to double up like a pocket knife to get into it. The sleepy middle-aged driver said he knew where the place was and set off northwards along the promenade at what, Marina thought privately, was quite a dangerous speed.

The car rattled and creaked but carried her safely to the *Furnas Langosteiras,* which was about three miles outside Estoril.

At first sight Marina thought her suspicions as to what Jean would find interesting were justified. The Café was very small, square and ugly. It was built off the road and as near as possible to some not very high

30

rocks over which the Atlantic rollers were breaking ferociously.

The taxi-man opened the door and said he would wait and because Marina was committed to seeing what there was to see, she got out.

There were a few chairs and tables set outside the building. There were half-a-dozen people sitting at them drinking coca-cola or coffee, and from the room inside there came an obvious smell of cooking.

Marina asked to see the Caves, wondering if perhaps Sybil had been mistaken in saying they existed. The young waiter understood and beckoning with his hand led her towards a rather dilapidated wooden gate against a rock at one side of the Café.

Marina followed him and saw rather to her surprise that there was a flight of very steep, rickety wooden steps leading straight down into the bowels of the earth. The waiter admonished her to be careful and she clutched thankfully at the none too steady hand rail and began to descend.

It grew darker, so dark that she turned her head enquiringly to ask how much further the steps went and then remembered that the few words she knew in Portuguese were not enough to cover such a question.

She turned back to continue the descent and as she did so her heel caught in the rough wood of the steps and she tripped. She gave a little cry and tried to save herself and half stumbled, half fell the remaining few feet.

She would have fallen to the ground if someone had not caught her. She felt a man's arms go round her. Felt the heavy impact as she fell against him and the sound which escaped her lips was half a cry and half a sigh of relief. Then a voice said in English:

"Are you all right?"

31

"Oh, I fell. Thank you for saving me!"

Marina answered him breathlessly, trying to regain her balance and at the same time extricate herself from his encircling arms.

She could see more clearly now. She had reached the floor of the cave and about twenty-five yards away was the opening on to the sea. The waves were splashing in, making a monotonous roar as they broke, retreated and broke again.

She saw that her saviour was a young man, tall, dark and broad-shouldered. He was smiling at her in a friendly fashion so that almost instinctively she smiled back.

"I'm sorry," she said. "It was silly of me not to be more careful. The steps are very precarious."

"It's lucky I caught you," he said. "The rock, I should imagine, could be very uncomfortable for anyone's knees."

He pointed downwards as he spoke and she saw that the floor was, in fact, nothing but rock, rough-hewn and pointed in places, so that, had he not caught her, there was every likelihood that the skin on both her knees would have been broken.

"You would think they might repair the steps, wouldn't you?" Marina said.

"Why should they? The place pays as it is," the young man said with a grin.

"That is obviously a dangerous philosophy. I might have sued them for damages."

"I believe litigation in this country," the young man replied, "takes years and years."

As he spoke, Marina realised he was not in fact English. He spoke the language perfectly; but there was just that perceptible difference in the accent which no foreigner can quite master.

He was good-looking, she decided, with something

about his thin face, clear-cut features and dark eyes that made him difficult to place. He was not Portuguese, she was certain of that, and he was certainly not French.

"Thank you very much, anyway," she said.

At that moment, the waiter who had been hovering near the mouth of the cave, snatched something from beneath the open boards over which the waves were breaking and carried it towards them.

"No langouste," he said in broken English, "but ver' fine crab."

It was an enormous one; its claws waving wildly in the air as it strove to free itself.

"It's rather big," Marina said.

"May we share it?" a voice asked behind her.

She glanced at the young man.

"I'm not really hungry," she said doubtfully. "It was only that I was told to see the caves."

"I came here for exactly the same reason," he answered. "I feel it would be rather feeble just to look and go away, don't you?"

"If you put it like that," Marina said with a smile, "I suppose we'll have to eat the crab."

Her new friend turned to the waiter and spoke rapidly in Portuguese. The boy seemed delighted, ran swiftly up the steps with the crab in his hand.

"There's no hurry," the stranger said to Marina. "I've told him we're hungry, but if I know anything of this sort of place, we'll be a good deal hungrier before our crab appears on the table."

Marina was looking at the waves.

"I think this place is rather frightening," she said. "It's so dark and one feels that the sea might surge in at any moment and then one would be trapped."

"It has that effect on me too," the young man answered. "Let's go upstairs to the sunshine."

"Yes, let's do that," Marina agreed with what she felt was an exaggerated sense of relief.

The dark, dampness of the cave had given her a feeling of claustrophobia and she felt almost trapped, so that she was glad as she scrambled up the rickety stairs to find the sunshine golden and the spray from the waves irridescent as it was flung high above the rocks.

They chose a table as far as possible from the Café itself. They sat for a moment saying nothing and watching the breakers. Then Marina realised that the young man's eyes were watching her face, and almost as a protection she said sharply:

"Perhaps we should introduce ourselves?"

"I was going to suggest the same thing," he answered. "My name is Carlos Ayelo."

"How d'you do?" Marina said, "and I'm Marina Marshall."

"You are English." It was a statement, not a question. Marina nodded.

"And you?"

There was a little pause before he answered.

"I'm South American."

"Oh!" The ejaculation slipped out before she could stop it "I wondered. Your English is very good but . . ." She hesitated for words.

"Not quite good enough," he supplied. "You didn't guess?"

"I'm afraid I didn't. I should have done as I've known quite a number of South Americans. Do you come from Brazil?"

"Let's talk about you."

She realised he was brushing her question aside deliberately.

"There's very little to tell," she answered evasively. "I'm here on a holiday and I work in London."

34

"And what work do you do?"

"Oh, I'm a secretary," Marina said quickly. "I'm a Private Secretary as a matter of fact to quite a big tycoon; that's why I can afford to spend quite a lot on my holidays."

She realised that she was being over-explanatory, at the same time she wanted to cover her tracks. She had not been sensible enough to think out an explanation for her presence in Portugal, not anticipating that anyone would ask her such an intimate question.

Having said she was a secretary, it had flashed through her mind that staying at the best hotel would require a little explanation unless she were earning a much bigger salary than the average secretary.

"Is your job interesting?" Carlos Ayelo asked.

"I suppose it is," Marina said, feeling that she was on dangerous ground and that it would be wisest to get off it. "Are you here on holiday?"

"You might put it that way," he answered. "I've never been in Portugal before, but I've heard about Estoril."

"That's why I'm here," Marina said. "I only arrived last night."

"Perhaps we had better explore Portugal together," the young man suggested.

Marina made no answer, but opened her handbag and took out her handkerchief. It was an unnecessary action and the man beside her gave a little laugh.

"Now I've shocked you—or should I say frightened you? I've been too precipitate! We work fast in my country. I think you are charming and very pretty, therefore I suggest I show you round unless, of course, you have someone more agreeable to escort you?"

He had a delightful and most persuasive way of

talking, and Marina, despite a resolution to be reserved, found herself smiling at him in reply.

"It sounds very simple and logical," she said, "but yet I feel we are in some way offending the conventions."

"What conventions?" Carlos Ayelo asked and shrugged his shoulders, "and if it comes to that, who's to know? I've no friends in Portugal and no relations. What about you?"

"Well, I suppose I'm in the same position," Marina answered.

"Then we're introduced," he said gaily. "You must admit it's a unique situation. Few people are so fortunate as to be introduced by a crab!"

"Let's hope it will be fortunate," Marina said almost mischievously. "I don't know that you're not a most dangerous character."

"A burglar, for instance," he asked, "trying to steal your jewels?"

"Well, you might be, at that," Marina said. "Or you might be a spy attempting to blow up the Portuguese Republic."

"What a wonderful idea!" Carlos agreed; "or I might be a kind of James Bond—isn't he your national hero?—trying to extort secrets from the wicked Russians."

"It's fascinating how many possibilities there are of what we might be," Marina said, "but actually, I'm only a secretary, and you?"

She asked the question directly looking at him as she spoke; but her inquisitiveness received no reward.

"I'm just unemployed at the moment."

"What sort of job d'you want?"

He put his hands as though to fend her off.

"Must we talk about work when I'm on holiday?" he enquired. "You don't want to talk about your boss, your typing or your shorthand or whatever you do. I don't want to discuss my employment. Let's talk about ourselves—our real selves. I want to know what you're thinking; what goes on behind those very beautiful eyes of yours."

"Would you be disappointed if I answered, 'Nothing'?" Marina enquired.

"Not disappointed. I just wouldn't believe you. You know, you are very romantic looking and, after all, this is the kind of thing that only happens in books, isn't it? Girl meets boy in unusual circumstances. In real life I'm much more likely to have caught a fat, middle-aged shopkeeper, or even her husband in my arms."

"And I should be thankful that you aren't a local fisherman smelling of fish and garlic; or perhaps the sanitary inspector making his annual report on the condition of the caves."

They laughed together at the fantasy and then, surprisingly quickly the crab appeared, split open and grilled; its flesh tender and sweet and so fresh that they could discern a taste of the sea in it.

They both ate greedily and for a moment said nothing; then Carlos wiped his mouth with a paper napkin and said with a sigh:

"I don't think I've ever tasted fish before today."

"I was thinking the same thing," Marina said. "How different the taste is when it has travelled for miles and been frozen!"

"We must come here again," he said. "Now the question is, where can we have lunch?"

"Don't talk about food at the moment," Marina pleaded.

"Very well, we will take some exercise," he agreed. "Just before I met you I was thinking of walking along the cliffs."

"I've just remembered I've a taxi waiting for me."

"Then tell him to wait until we come back," Carlos suggested. "A walk is a good idea; a little way along the coast you'll find a profusion of wild flowers. I've a feeling you would like that."

"How did you know?" Marina asked.

"You remind me of a flower," he said simply, and somehow the words were not exaggerated because he said them.

"What sort of flower?" she asked curiously.

"I was wondering about that myself," he said. "I suppose most people would say an orchid, because you are so unusual, exquisite, a little exotic. But an orchid is not good enough for you. It has no scent. It's too artificial. No, I think you are a camelia, a perfect, unblemished camelia opening its smooth petals to the sun and being in every way quite unlike the more ordinary humdrum flowers around it."

"You're flattering me," Marina said.

"As a matter of fact I'm not," he said in an almost casual tone. "I'm not usually so high-flown in my ideas or my compliments. I think you're rather an unusual person, Marina."

She stiffened a little because he had called her by her Christian name, then told herself she was being absurd. After all, she had allowed herself to be picked up so easily by a young man, she had eaten a meal with someone to whom she had never been introduced—she must expect a little familiarity. And really, what did it matter?

Tomorrow she would very likely go back to England and never see him again. At least he had dispelled that feeling of loneliness which had persisted even when she was enjoying the sunshine and her walk along the plage.

"Well?" he asked.

38

"Well, what?" she replied.

"Say it," he said. "I'm waiting to hear you don't approve of me calling you by your Christian name; that you're not quite certain you haven't been over rash or over hasty sitting down to eat with me after so short an acquaintance."

For a moment Marina stared at him, then she laughed.

"Are you a thought reader?" she asked.

"Sometimes," he answered enigmatically.

"Then don't read my thoughts," she said. "I don't like it."

"Don't be stuffy!" he retorted. "Forget you're English."

"I'm not entirely English," she said, because she resented the implication of being stuffy. "I'm half-American."

"North, of course," he said with a little smile.

"Of course!" she answered. "Or rather South of the North."

"Well, that may account for it," he said almost as though he were thinking aloud. "I felt that you couldn't be typically English, and yet where else would you find a woman with such a complexion and such hair?"

"I'm English enough to feel uncomfortable when you pay me compliments," Marina said.

"Why do they let you girls grow up so *gauche?* You should learn to accept them gracefully, like a Frenchwoman."

"We certainly don't angle for them like the French do," Marina snapped.

He threw back his head and laughed.

"I belive I've really annoyed you," he said. "Perhaps I've got under your skin at last. You're very self-assured, Miss Marshall. How many jobs have you had, to walk about as though the world was only dirt beneath your feet?"

"You've been reading women's magazines," Marina said "that's the sort of cliché they employ."

"And why not? We're living a perfect magazine story which any woman would want to buy," he answered. "Can't you see the title? 'The Cave of Loneliness' or, 'They Were Strangers and He Held Her in His Arms'?"

"You're ridiculous!" Marina said. "What about that walk?"

"I'll pay the bill," he said.

She started guiltily and realised she had not thought that being out of work he might not have the money for such extravagance.

"No, please, this is my treat," she said quickly, taking up her bag.

She knew without looking up there was a frown between his eyes as he said:

"Are you insulting me?"

"Now, don't be silly," she said. "I'm a stranger to you and while its rather fun to do things together, I insist on paying my share. I can afford it, I promise you."

"So can I," he answered. "And damn your independence. If you think I'm going to stand for a Dutch treat you're very much mistaken."

"But I insist," Marina said.

She was quite certain that he must be poor, otherwise he would not be so insistent in paying for her.

In answer Carlos got up from the table and walked into the café. She saw him pay the bill, leaving a tip for the waiter, and then come back towards her.

"You're making things very difficult for me," Marina said, slowly putting the notes she had taken out of her case back in their proper compartment.

"Why? because I like women to be feminine and dependent and not aggressively intelligent?"

"Oh, you're being old-fashioned. What I believe is called a 'square'," Marina said.

"Then I shall continue to be a square," he said. "I've never yet let a woman pay for me and I don't intend to start now."

"Very well," Marina conceded, "but if you have to cut your holiday short because of gross extravagance, don't blame me."

"I won't," he answered. "Come on. We'll tell the taxi to wait. We'll come back to him in about an hour's time."

"That, too, is extravagant," Marina said, "If you sent him away we could doubtless telephone for another."

"Oh, the English with their sensible practicability," he groaned, "always the inevitable 'Take this 'bus from the corner, it's a penny cheaper if you do'!"

"How d'you know so much about the English?" Marina asked.

"I was at school in England, as it happens," Carlos answered.

"Oh!"

For a moment Marina was nonplussed. He had been in England. He might not only have heard of her but have recognised her.

"I've never been back," Carlos was saying, "I've always meant to go."

Marina felt relief seep over her. Just for one moment she had felt a horrifying suspicion that he had recognised her and had scraped up an acquaintance because he had known who she was.

It had happened to her before. There was the young man at the carnival who had penetrated her disguise and who had attached himself to her assiduously, or the young man who had too casually at the bridge club invited her to make a four.

There had been men who had sought acquaintance on ships or aeroplanes, in casinos, at private parties, and all too soon she had learnt that they were fortune hunters, gigolos or international playboys who were all attracted not by Marina Martyn but by only one thing—her money.

"Tell me about England," Carlos was saying at her side. "Do the Houses of Parliament still want cleaning? Does Buckingham Palace look just as smug as it always did? And are the Bond Street shops as full of expensive presents which no one can afford?"

Marina answered him in the same vein, and as they walked along by the sea to the left of them, the wild flowers on the right stretching away under the trunks of strange, stunted trees, she found herself laughing with an incredible gaiety at almost everything they said to one another.

Carlos had an amusing way of asking questions; of turning the most mundane thing into something impish and making her laugh at his experiences in England.

He told her how he taught himself to speak perfect English by recording his voice on a tape recorder and noting his mistakes.

"But why did you take so much trouble?" Marina asked him.

"I don't like foreigners," he said.

They both went into peals of laughter because it seemed such a ridiculous thing to say. They were still laughing when they walked back to the taxi.

"Now are you hungry?" Carlos asked.

"Ravenous," Marina replied.

"Very well, then," he said. "We will go and eat

at a little place I know where there is a balcony in the sunshine with wistaria climbing up it."

"It sounds romantic," Marina said, "but is the food good?"

"If it isn't, we'll go somewhere else," he said.

The way he said it made her wonder once again what he was and what he did. He had an air of command about him in spite of the fact that he was prepared to play the fool.

She was quite certain he was an executive in some way; and yet, if he was head of a firm, why should he have said he was unemployed and wandering about Portugal alone? Perhaps, she thought, there was big business lurking behind it all somewhere.

He didn't seem a playboy. There was too purposeful an air about him, and if he had been one, she was quite certain he would not have been alone on this holiday. The playboys of this world would feel lost without their casinos and yachts and speed-boats and their expensive cars. "He's rather a mystery," Marina thought to herself.

After she had washed her hands in the cloakroom of the little restaurant she went upstairs to find Carlos sitting on the balcony looking out to sea, chin resting in his hands, with a far-away expression in his eyes.

Just for a moment she watched him without his seeing her. Then he got to his feet. There was a smile on his lips and she knew she had caught him off guard, and yet it had got her no farther in her understanding of what he was or where he had come from.

The lunch was good. Because they were hungry they enjoyed every mouthful. They drank the sparkling red Mateus which Carlos said was the best wine

43

of Portugal and which Marina had never sampled before.

Then as the other guests in the restaurant paid their bills and drifted away, they sat looking out to sea with the scent of wistaria in their nostrils, and they talked.

Not particularly of themselves, but what they thought of life and love and people and God and all the other things two young people talk about when they are getting to know each other and finding out that life is like an exciting road winding through valleys and mountains, forests and towns.

"When I first saw you," Carlos said, "I thought you were very lovely; now I'm entranced by your brain."

"I don't think anyone has ever told me that before," Marina said.

"Why should they," Carlos replied. "I expect their concern has been whether you could add up two and two and make it four—or if you knew the quickest and best way to get to Timbuctoo—or how to work a computer. It's not that part of your brain I'm concerned with but the part which thinks today what you're to become tomorrow."

"We've talked about so many things this afternoon, I'd much rather you didn't draw conclusions about me," Marina said almost defensively.

"Now I'm frightening you," Carlos said. "Why do you want to be unapproachable? Why do you want to build a wall around yourself?"

"Oh, I suppose as a protection against getting hurt," Marina said.

"So you've been hurt," he said softly. "I thought so."

"A long time ago," Marina said. "It's not worth thinking about it, and yet in a way it has left its mark. Or rather, it's made me want things that perhaps I'll never find."

44

"Love?" he asked, perceptively.

She picked up her bag.

"I don't want to answer that question."

"There's no need," he said. "Shall I thought-read again and tell you what you're thinking?"

"No," she said quickly.

He took no notice.

"You're thinking I'm too perceptive. I see too much, therefore you're afraid of me," he said. "You're right, I do see . . ."

He paused and then went on in a deeper tone:

"I see a girl who is trying to hide behind a sophisticated, polished veneer. But at heart she is only a child, a child who believes in all the beautiful things of life, all the things that everyone wants, but is too proud and too obstinate to say so. She wants love—and what woman doesn't—a love which is beautiful because it is selfless, an ecstacy because it is divine. A love that is wonderful because it's human."

He stopped, and after a second went on, his eyes smiling:

"Of course, you want love. It'll make your heart beat faster and the breath come more quickly between your lips. You want love that moves within you like a leaping flame, and you know that, sooner or later, it will set the whole of you on fire."

His voice was almost hypnotic. Violently Marina pushed back her chair so that the legs scraped on the stone floor.

"Stop!" she cried. "You're being too imaginative."

She stood looking straight at him, her face was white and tense.

"Oh, my dear," he said softly, "I didn't mean to hurt you."

"I think we've talked long enough," Marina said quietly. "It's time we went. Everyone else has gone."

"You won't gain anything by running away," he said.

"It's time to go," Marina reiterated.

Without waiting for his reply she walked from the balcony into the restaurant, across the small room and down the stairs.

As she went, she felt the blood pounding at her temples, and a sudden, strange anger within her.

"How dare he?" she asked herself.

She knew that he had put his finger unerringly on a nerve which throbbed and ached because she could not deny the truth of what he had said.

"I must go back to my hotel; there's no point in my seeing him again," she told herself.

Even as she thought it, she knew such an action was impossible. It would be running away and she knew in her heart of hearts that she couldn't run away from Carlos—not yet.

3

"Happy?" Carlos asked the question softly, and Marina smiled back at him.

She was not surprised, for she had been thinking that very moment how happy she was. She had grown used to his reading her thoughts, even anticipating what she was going to say.

She had never in her whole life met a man who was so perceptive or in fact so sensitive to her every mood. It had for Marina been two days of almost perfect happiness.

Carlos had shown her Lisbon; the Church of the Madre de Dios, the glories of the Cathedral at Belem; and then they had taken a car and driven out into the country to look at the empty palaces where once the Kings of Portugal had reigned in splendour.

Although at first Marina was surprised at how much Carlos knew about the history of a country to which he didn't belong, she had grown accustomed to finding he had an extensive knowledge of almost everything, of history, architecture, paintings, even of geology; and because she liked to listen to him talking in his soft voice, the hours passed so quickly and it seemed to her that almost before the morning was past night had fallen.

Now their second day was finished and they were sitting in a little night club off the Alta Vera listening to the strange melancholy sounds of the fado.

"You think you're going to hate it," Marina said,

"and then it has a strange fascination. You want to hear more."

"That's love as the Portuguese see it," Carlos answered.

"They must love to be unhappy," she commented.

"Not exactly unhappy," he said, "but love should always be serious."

It wasn't the answer she had expected. It wasn't the answer anyone in her set in London would have given, because men like Victor were always seeking amusement, always wanting to be entertained; therefore love which was serious was to them usually a bore.

"What exactly do you mean by serious?" she asked curiously.

"I mean," Carlos replied, "that real love between a man and a woman can never be a quiet, placid thing, a pastel portrait of nondescript emotions. It must be strong, violent, fiery; something which sweeps one off one's feet, something which is irresistible."

"I wonder if it really exists like that?" Marina said. "I've never known it."

"No, I can see that," he answered.

"See it?" she asked.

"But of course," he answered. "I can see it in your face, in your eyes, in the movement of your lips. You're a sleeping beauty, unawakened, the flower that is still in bud."

"How glorious that sounds," she exclaimed and laughed.

But as she did so her laughter seemed out of place and she realised that Carlos was deadly serious.

"Someone will one day awaken you," he said. "I wish it could be me."

For a moment Marina thought she had not heard him aright and to her look of enquiry he answered:

48

"Oh, I'm only a ship that passes in the night. A holiday friend, whom one remembers only by the snapshot. Don't you realise that?"

"I don't think I've thought about it," Marina told him, not exactly truthfully.

"Perhaps one day you'll think back on this time," he said not looking at her, "and say, 'I wonder where Carlos is now? It was great fun while it lasted.'"

"That sounds as though you are going to die," Marina said more for something to say than for any other reason.

She was nonplussed. She had never expected the conversation to take this turn. She had never for that matter imagined any man would tell her she was but a transitory unimportant thing in his life. That had always been her prerogative. She had always been the one to insist that a flirtation or a love affair was something gay and charming to which no one should attach any thought of permanence.

"No, I'm not going to die," Carlos said slowly. "Not if I can help it; but I'm afraid."

"Afraid? Afraid of what?" Marina enquired.

"Of getting too fond of you," he said simply. "Oh, Marina, I've been happy today too. I never realised sightseeing could be so much fun. Wandering around those castles and palaces with parties of gaping tourists became, somehow, the most amusing thing that had ever happened, just because you were there."

"I enjoyed it too," Marina said quietly.

"I knew that," he answered. "Had you been bored, even for one instant, I should have known. We were close to each other, remember?"

She looked away from him because now his eyes were on her she was afraid of their expression.

She was remembering a moment in the pink Palace at Quelez when they had stood together in the lovely music room while the tourists who were with them had clumped away after the guide.

There were mirrors on every wall as if it were attempting to be a miniature Versailles, and in them Marina had seen herself and Carlos reflected and rereflected, winding away into infinity, her fair hair reaching just to his shoulders, his dark head bent towards her.

"I think the last Kings and Queens to live here must have been happy," she said almost involuntarily.

Because of her own happiness the whole Palace seemed enchanted.

"Perhaps we lived here in another incarnation," he answered. "I almost have the feeling of home-coming."

Without explanations, because they both knew what the other wanted, they had not followed the tourists further round the Palace. Instead they had gone into the garden where the fountains were playing in the ornamental canal and the spring flowers were raising their yellow heads beside the green lawns.

"It's so beautiful," Marina breathed.

"And so are you," Carlos said.

It was hardly necessary for him to speak the words because the look in his eyes was enough.

She felt a strange feeling beneath her breast at that moment and she felt it again now as he put out his hand and took hers.

The touch of his fingers had a strange effect on her. Then he turned her palm upwards and looked down at it.

"Shall I tell your fortune?" he asked.

She wanted to say "No" feeling he might be too perceptive. Because she felt it would sound absurd, she left her hand on his, only wondering for a moment whether he might see too much.

"What shall I tell you?" he asked looking down at the lines etched into the soft pink of her palm.

"Can you really tell fortunes?" Marina asked.

"I can tell yours," he answered fiercely. "You'll marry someone charming, rich and important and you'll grace his fine house and the high position he will hold in the country. Everyone will admire you and look up to you. You'll be what they call the 'Lady of the Manor'. Does that content you?"

It seemed to Marina that he almost spat the words at her.

Now she snatched her hand away from his and said sharply:

"Why are you trying to be unkind to me? Do you think that's the sort of life I'd want?"

"It's the sort of life every woman wants," he answered. "Security, a complacent husband, no worries."

"I should hate it," Marina retorted and wondered why her voice sounded strange. "I want more from life than money and position, but perhaps you don't understand that."

"Now you're being unkind to me," Carlos said, "Oh, my darling, don't you understand I'm jealous of this unknown man, this husband who'll give you all the things you deserve."

There was a sudden throb in his voice which made Marina feel shy.

"Then why talk about him?" she asked. "He doesn't yet exist."

"Hell! That's what's so damnable—he will," Carlos exclaimed. "I can't imagine why your're not married already."

"I've never met what my Nanny used to call 'Mr Right'," Marina said. "There've been quite a lot of 'Mr Wrongs'."

51

"I knew that without your telling me about them," Carlos said grimly. "Of course men will want you to marry them—thank God! I shan't be there to see it."

Before Marina could answer him—and indeed she could find no answer to such a peculiar statement— he snapped his fingers to the waiter and called for the bill.

He paid for it and they moved away from the night club out into the soft darkness of the night. It was not cold and Marina felt that she hardly needed the stole she had slipped round her shoulders.

They walked a little way up the cobbled street. There were restaurants, bars and small night clubs every few yards. They walked without speaking; then as they came to a cross-roads a taxi came bearing down on them: Carlos hailed it and helped Marina in.

"Are we going to the hotel?" Marina asked.

"Not yet," he answered.

He gave the taxi driver some instructions and sinking back on the seat he took Marina's hand in his and tucked it through his arm. It was a gesture of comfort and companionship, and yet Marina felt an almost uncontrollable impulse to sit nearer to him and almost invite him to put his arm round her.

She was puzzled and perturbed by his last words at the table. He had spoken as if he might be leaving at any moment. If he was going away, where was he going? Was there the possibility that she'd never see him again?

She longed to ask him for the answer, but she had learnt already in the last two days that he was extremely skillful at evading any direct question about himself.

She had tried again and again to catch him out;

to make him tell her about his family, his work, his experiences: anything that might give her a lead, so that she could know more about him. But always she came up against a blank wall.

Now after they had driven for some moments, she broke the silence, saying:

"You cheated over my future. You didn't really look at the lines on my hand. You only made up what you expected to see."

"I didn't want to look," he said. "I might see things that would really make me unhappy."

"Why must you be so mysterious? Why do you talk of going away? And why do you talk in a manner which makes me feel you might be going away tomorrow?"

"Perhaps I shall have to," he said. "I don't know. That's the answer: I don't know, Marina."

"But it's ridiculous," she said. "We all know things about ourselves which we may not want others to know; that's a different thing altogether. But you must know."

"I don't," he answered. "I've no plans and no idea what tomorrow might bring."

"Now you're being mysterious again," Marina said with a sigh.

"I've told you," he said harshly, "this is a holiday interlude. Isn't that enough?"

Marina felt suddenly shaken by his refusal to confide in her.

"Of course it is," she said coldly. "You must forgive me for appearing inquisitive. I'm not really being impertinent."

She slipped her arm from his and moved a little away from him into the corner of the taxi.

"Oh, you ridiculous child!" he said. "Of course you're inquisitive and bursting with curiosity."

She saw his face, laughing at her. Now his arms came out and drew her close to him again.

"You're just being very feminine and I like it. In fact I like you to be human and unpretentious, just as you are, but I still can't tell you anything about myself."

"But why not?" Marina asked before she could prevent the words slipping from between her lips.

"Shall I say I'm an adventurer? A man who's wanted by Interpol? A spy with the plans of a new type of bomb in my pocket? You'd respect me then for keeping silent."

"I just don't believe that. Spies who have plans of worldshattering bombs don't go down into caves to look for crabs," Marina answered.

He laughed at that; and then the taximan, who could have overheard all their conversation, said from the front seat:

"Is this where you wish to stop, Senhor?"

Marina looked out of the window. She had been so intent on their conversation she had not noticed where they were going. Now she saw they had climbed high out of the town, up a winding road which led them to the yellow battlements of Castello de S. Jorge, which crowned the hilltop and dominated the centre of Lisbon.

She had seen the Castle in the daytime and knew it had been built on the site of an old Moorish fortress and that it was this strongpoint, watching over the Tagus, that the English crusaders had helped to capture from the Moors.

"Why have we come here?" she asked Carlos, but she was delighted at the idea because even from the taxi she could see the lights of Lisbon twinkling like a fairyland below them.

"Come and look," he suggested and helped her out.

They walked along the battlements in the darkness, looking down on the twisting river towards the bay where the ships were moored with their green and red lights.

There was no wind. It seemed to Marina that there was the tang of the sea in the air mingled with the scent of wild flowers growing on the sides of the castle.

They were entirely alone up here away from the noise and bustle of the city, their only companion the quietness of the old moss-covered stones which had lived through so much history and so much bloodshed.

They came to a seat and sat down looking towards the town; and then slowly, deliberately, without haste Carlos took Marina in his arms.

She knew this was the moment for which she had been waiting and she made no pretence of not surrendering her lips to him as he demanded.

She felt the first touch of his mouth, gentle yet insistent. She thought she had never been kissed quite like this before, and then the kiss which had started so softly became harder, hungrier and more possessive. She felt the passion rise within him and knew something within her responded almost simultaneously.

Their mouths clung together and in that moment it seemed to Marina as though fireworks crashed overhead and the lights from the town rose to explode around them.

This was ecstasy, a thrill, a joy she had never experienced in her whole life. She felt she couldn't breathe, and yet breath was unnecessary; she was floating upwards into a realm of glory beyond anything she had ever known.

Only when Carlos took his lips from hers did she realise that she was trembling, and the rapture he had aroused in her made her turn her head and hide her eyes against his shoulder.

He did not speak, only touched her hair very gently and she felt herself quiver. She tried not to be swept away by the tide of emotions coursing through her.

Quite suddenly he rose to his feet. She felt her hands go out to stop him, but he had moved out of reach. He stood with his back to her against the battlement, looking towards the river.

Marina felt as though her voice had died in her throat, the sweetness, the wonder of that kiss seemed still to hold her spellbound; and then, after a long time, she managed to articulate his name:

"Carlos!"

It was a cry, a plea in the voice of a child who had been awakened in the night.

"Forgive me."

It wasn't what she had expected him to say.

"What for?" she asked, still speaking to his back, his silhouette square and dark against the sky.

"I shouldn't have done that."

His voice sounded suddenly empty, almost weary.

"Why not?"

He turned round to her then and stood looking down at her. There was a pale moon lighting up the sky and he could see her face clearly as she raised it towards his.

Her eyes were dark and questioning. Her mouth was soft, full and relaxed, the lips of a woman who had been kissed and who had kissed in return. A little pulse was throbbing in her throat and for a moment his hands went out as though he would touch her, then he dropped them to his sides.

"I'm leaving tomorrow," he said.

"But why—must you go?"

Marina was surprised even as she spoke at the distress in her own voice.

"I've got to go. Don't you understand? Aren't you woman enough to know what is happening?"

"Does it matter?" she asked almost pitifully. "Are you married?"

Somehow the idea had never come to her until this moment. She had been so certain that he was free like herself, untrammelled, unchained.

"No, I'm not married," he said. "As I've already told you, this for both of us is a holiday, an interlude, a chance encounter."

"And now it's over," Marina said. "Why?"

"Can't you understand? Because it has ceased to be any of these things. I told you love was serious. This is serious, too serious. I've got to go."

"For your sake or for mine?" Marina asked.

"If I was dishonest," he answered, "I should say for your's, but if I told the truth, I'm thinking of myself. I daren't let myself love you. You don't understand and I can't explain. It's something that mustn't happen."

He turned away from her again and now Marina put her hands up to her eyes.

Where was her pride? she asked herself. This man told her he did not want her. Why didn't she get up and go? Why didn't she tell him she, too, was leaving tomorrow, that she was going back to England? She hoped they would both have happy memories of the amusing time they had had together. And then she thought desperately she couldn't let him go like this. It was absurd, ridiculous.

She got to her feet and went to his side.

"Aren't we being a little over-dramatic?"

The words instead of sounding almost severe sounded only breathless and a little frightened.

"Are we?" he asked. "Perhaps you're right. Let me kiss you again and then you can tell me it's charming, delightful, not of the least importance."

He didn't move, but Marina instinctively took a step backwards.

"You see," he said, "you daren't trust me. Or is it of yourself you're frightened?"

"I don't understand," Marina said. "Oh, Carlos, why can't you make things simple for me?"

"Because there's nothing simple about touching you," he answered. "I knew it was mad to come up here tonight, and yet I couldn't resist the idea of being here with you."

He paused, then as she didn't speak, he continued:

"The day before we'd met I came here alone. I sat on this very seat. I looked at the ships going across the sea towards the west, towards my country and as I watched them go I suddenly felt there was someone here beside me, someone who meant something in my life, someone who held in her little hands the strings of my heart. Of course I thought I was being imaginative. Yet tonight, when we left the night club, I knew I must bring you here."

"Do I hold the strings of your heart?" Marina asked, her voice was hardly above a whisper.

"Yes!" Carlos said almost brutally. "You've made me say it, haven't you? All right, I love you. Or rather, I'm beginning to love you far too much for my own peace of mind. I can't risk any more. Even now, I'm not certain if I can bring myself to break

58

away. I'm telling myself it's for your sake; you mustn't be hurt."

"Hurt by whom?" Marina asked.

"By me, if you like," Carlos replied. "I can mean nothing to you."

He put out his arm and pointed.

"You see those ships down there? You see that one moving out in the bay? That's me. I'm moving out of your life quietly, and I hope, with dignity. I've got to go."

Marina didn't speak, but he took her by the arm.

"Come," he said, "we're going back. Don't make it worse, Marina; there's nothing more either of us can say."

There was a note of command in his voice and she bit back the questions that were trembling on her lips, forced back the tears that were not far from her eyes.

She walked back towards the taxi, and on the way she told herself this could not be happening to her. No man had ever dared to turn down Marina Martyn; but now, this man whom she hardly knew was going to leave her—leave her with his kiss on her lips and the feeling in her heart that he was already an inseparable part of her.

The taxi descended the hill; they sat in silence. They passed through the old part of the town and reached the wider and more open roads which led towards Estoril.

It seemed to Marina as though their silence embraced them like a black cloud. She couldn't move; she couldn't even think. She just knew that something terrible was happening which she could do nothing about.

She tried to sort things out in her own mind, to force herself to reason sensibly and coherently; it was impossible. She could only feel her body still tingling from his kiss and the unshed tears behind her eyes because he had told her he must go.

They were already moving along the road bordering the sea which led to Estoril. Out in the open bay the lights of the fishing vessels, overhead the stars were shining.

"It's a night for love," Marina thought, and yet it was passing her by.

She wanted to cry out, to protest, only an iron self-control prevented her from throwing herself into his arms and begging him to stay and if he could not do that, to kiss her again.

"What has happened to me?" she asked herself despairingly and knew the answer even though she dared not say it to herself.

They drew up at the hotel. Carlos paid the taxi.

"I shall walk back from here," he said and followed her into the brightly lighted hallway.

She looked up at him pleadingly. Were they going to say "Good-bye" here?

"I'll see you to the lift," he said.

His face was stern and uncompromising. He didn't look directly at her.

The lift was to the right a little way along the hall. Carlos pressed the bell and they stood without speaking. And it seemed to Marina that now at last there was nothing to say.

She clenched her hands together and felt the nails biting into her palms. She mustn't break down; she mustn't make a scene here near the reception desk where people were passing in and out almost within earshot.

The lift came down with a clang. She heard the porter pull open the iron gate, then the outer door opened and he stood to one side to admit her.

Carlos held out his hand.

"Good night, Marina," he said. "And thank you."

She put her hand in his, knowing that her fingers were cold and feeling the strength of his close over them. Then, as she looked up at him his face changed almost fantastically.

He was facing towards the entrance hall, and the sudden sound of someone speaking made his eyes glance for a moment from her. She felt him start; saw a strange, almost frightening expression change his eyes and his mouth; then almost before she could realise what was happening he had turned sharply and pulled her into the lift.

"Don't wait!" he said commandingly to the porter. "We're in a hurry."

The man shut the door and pulled to the iron gates.

"What floor, Senhor?" he enquired.

Marina knew that the pressure of Carlos's fingers on hers was a signal for her to speak.

"The third," she said.

They shot up. At the third floor Carlos hurried her out of the lift.

"Which way?" he asked sharply.

"This," she answered, pointing to the left.

She found herself almost running to keep up with him. They stopped at the door of her room and she took the key from her bag. He snatched it from her and fitted it into the lock and to her surprise, almost pushed her into the room, shutting the door behind them and locking it.

"What's the matter?" Marina enquired.

"Listen," he answered, "some men arrived while we were talking. They may have seen me, I'm not sure. If they did, they will enquire of the lift-man which room we've gone to."

61

He broke off speaking and walked to the window, pulling back the curtain to look at the sheer drop to the garden below.

He put his hand to his forehead.

"I shouldn't have come up with you," he said. "It was mad. I should have gone down the corridor and slipped out by another door. Good God, Marina, I don't want to involve you in this!"

"In what?" Marina asked. "Who are these men? What do they want of you?"

"I can't answer that," he said. "But I'll try and get away. I must go at once."

"But are you in danger—really in danger?" Marina asked. "Then, of course, you can't leave. Stay here, they'll never find you and if they do—"

"No, no," he said. "I've made a fool of myself already. I'm sorry, darling, I love you far too much to let you play any part in this unpleasantness."

He put his arms around her and laid his cheek against hers.

"God bless you," he said softly. "Take care of yourself always. I shall never forget you."

Marina put her arms around him and held him close.

"I don't understand," she said. "You can't go. I won't let you!"

"I've got to," he said. "Already I've done a damned silly thing. Good-bye, my Sweetheart."

He disengaged her hands, kissed her lightly on the forehead, and turned towards the door. As he did so, there was a sudden knock. They both stood paralysed, staring at the locked door. Neither of them moved. The knock came again. Carlos signalled to Marina and she called out:

"Who's there?"

"Will the Senhora please open the door?"

The answer was in faulty English; the voice was authoritative.

Marina pointed towards the cupboard and Carlos tiptoed over towards it. She waited until he was inside then crossing the room she unlocked the door and opened it little more than a crack.

"What is it?" she asked. "I'm going to bed."

There were two men standing outside. They wore dark raincoats and slouch hats and looked like stage detectives.

"Your pardon, Senhora," said the elder of the two men. "We wish to see your passport. Will you fetch it for us, please."

His eyes shifted as he spoke, to the room behind her and Marina knew without being told that if she left the door they would force their way into the room.

"My passport has already been seen at the Reception desk," she said. "There's nothing wrong with it."

There was something about his manner, his air of aggression which would have made Mary Marshall, if she had been standing there, obey him. She wouldn't have been able to stand up against that show of authority and officialdom. She would have fetched her passport because she would have felt that there was nothing else she could do.

But Marina wasn't used to being ordered about. Behind the men in the passage she saw one of the clerks from the Reception desk. He had obviously been showing a newcomer to one of the bedrooms, and now, as he turned towards the lift, Marina called to him:

"Senhor!" she said, "come here a moment if you please."

Her voice was in its own way as authoritative as

63

that of the strange man who had commanded her to show him her passport and the clerk came towards her.

"Can I help you, Senhora?" he enquired politely.

"These gentlemen demand to see my passport at this time of night," Marina replied. "Is that usual in this hotel or in this country? It has never happened to me before."

The reception clerk looked surprised.

"Your passport, Senhora?" he questioned.

He turned to the men and asked them a question in Portuguese. The younger of the two men, who had stood a little behind the other, took a step forward. Marina knew in that split second that the reception clerk was in danger.

How she knew it she was not sure, she just knew intuitively that the smell of danger was there and something was about to happen.

Without thinking what she was doing she intervened.

"I think I saw Senor Vermilio a moment ago on this floor," she said to the reception clerk. "If you will look round the corner, he will doubtless be there. Ask him to come here immediately."

The clerk turned his head, moving a few steps backward so that he could look down the passage. The two men in raincoats glanced at each other.

"There is some mistake," the elder one muttered. "I apologise. We will make enquiries downstairs."

They moved rapidly away, almost before the reception clerk realised what was happening.

"Please go after them," Marina said to him. "I think they have no right in this hotel."

"I'll do that, Senhora," the clerk said and hurried down the corridor after the men who had now almost reached the lift.

Marina closed the door and locked it. She felt suddenly shaky, as if she had passed through a gruelling experience.

As she stood there holding on to the door-handle, Carlos stepped from the wardrobe.

"Thank you. You were wonderful," he said. "Now hurry, we've got to leave at once."

"Leave at once," Marina repeated. "What do you mean? The men have gone."

"D'you really believe that?" he asked. "They'll be back within the next twenty minutes or so. Hurry! You can't pack; you can't take any clothes. Just put what you want in that case."

He pointed to Marina's small white vanity case in which she carried her cosmetics.

"But I can't come with you," she said.

"You've got to," he answered. "They've seen you with me and they'll stick at nothing to find out what you know; and even if you know nothing that won't stop their trying to force it out of you."

There was such conviction in his tone that Marina felt herself shiver.

"Are they really dangerous?" she asked.

"As dangerous as hell," he replied. "Come on; don't waste time. You've got to trust me. I didn't mean it to come to this. But it's too late now."

Almost in a haze as though she was too bemused to argue with him Marina thrust her powder, lotions and creams into the fitted compartments of her vanity case. There was just room for it to hold a toothbrush.

While she was doing this Carlos took from the wardrobe a little plain grey coat and skirt which she sometimes wore for travelling. She hadn't really realised until she had unpacked that she had brought it with her.

"Put that on," he commanded, throwing it on the bed, "and hurry—for God's sake hurry!"

Marina was infected by his sense of urgency. He stood with his back to her looking out of the window as she changed the black cocktail dress of guipure lace which she had worn for dinner for the plain coat and skirt with its white silk blouse. It had been cut by a master hand and the severity of it became her fair pink and white looks. But she didn't have a moment to glance at herself in the mirror.

"You must have a coat," Carlos said, as he realised she was ready.

"Yes, there's one somewhere," Marina answered.

He slipped it from a hanger and put it over her shoulders.

"Now then," he said. "I'll open the door and don't stand looking about the corridor, make for the service stairs. They must be somewhere towards the back of the building."

"How d'you know?" Marina wanted to ask, but there was no time for questions.

He turned out the light and very, very gently edged the door open; then, as he saw there was no one outside, he put out his hand and took hers.

They hurried across the landing and down the corridor which led to the back of the hotel. As they turned the corner a waiter carrying a tray came through a door marked "Service".

They clattered down three flights of stone stairs and found themselves in a yard in which were innumerable dustbins and several vans. It was dark and rather smelly.

In the shadows Carlos drew a small torch from his pocket. He opened the door of the first van.

"No key," he whispered.

Then he looked in a smaller one.

He beckoned to Marina and helped her in, then got in the driver's seat. There was a smell of fresh bread which told Marina what the van usually carried.

Now they were moving out of the yard through an open gate onto the high road.

"Where're we going?" she asked.

"The railway station," he answered.

"But where then? Oh, Carlos, this is so mad."

"Don't talk to me," he said. "I've got to concentrate on driving. If we don't get away now we're done for."

He put his foot down on the accelerator and Marina realised that at the pace they were soon travelling it was absolutely essential that he should concentrate.

He drove down the broad, now comparatively empty streets which led them back to Lisbon. Carlos seemed to know the way and only hesitated once or twice before finally they drew up outside the railway station. He parked the van and taking her once again by the hand ran toward the booking office.

"What time does the next express leave?" he asked in Portuguese.

The man glanced at the clock behind him.

"The Paris Express will be leaving in three minutes," he answered.

"Two first class tickets, please."

Carlos slammed down the money, picked up the tickets and they ran to the platform.

The train was crowded. There seemed to be crowds of people seeing their friends off. Carlos wrenched open the door of the last coach just as the whistle blew and the engine started to chug its way slowly out of the station. The train was actually moving as he pulled Marina inside and shut the door behind them.

"We've done it," he said breathlessly. There was a note of triumph in his voice.

They started on their way along the train towards the first class compartments. The third were crowded Marina noticed and even when they got to the first class coaches, there didn't seem to be much room.

Carlos found a Sleeping Car attendant.

"I want two sleepers," he said and as he spoke he drew a note from his pocket and slipped it into the man's hand.

He spoke in French and Marina saw with surprise that the sleeping-car attendant was a Frenchman. It was typical of Carlos, she thought, to notice the man's nationality and to be able to speak to him in his own language.

"I cannot give you what I haven't got, Monsieur," the man expostulated.

"There must be one that's empty," Carlos said almost coaxingly.

"Well, there is one, as it happens," the attendant said grudgingly. "But the gentleman will be coming back at any moment from the Dining Car. I don't know what I'm going to say to him."

"I'm sure you'll think of something very clever," Carlos said.

Another note changed hands and now the sleeping car attendant led them to the centre of the car and opened the door of No. 5.

"*Voilà, Monsieur, Madame.* I hope you'll pass a pleasant night."

He raised his cap politely and went out, shutting the door behind him. Marina let out a sigh of relief and sat down on the bottom bunk.

"We're safe!" she said. "If we had come only a minute later we would have had to wait at the station."

"Don't speak too soon," Carlos abruptly admonished her. "It's unlucky."

Marina put out her hand.

"Don't frighten me," she said, "not any more than I've been frightened already. Please, Carlos, tell me what all this is about?"

4

Carlos did not answer and Marina looked up at him questioningly. The expression on his face, she decided, was one of anxiety. She smiled encouragingly.

"It's all right now," she said, "We're safe!"

"Are we?" he replied. "I've a feeling—" He stopped. "I'm trying to work things out."

After a pause he continued; almost beneath his breath:

"They knew I was in Estoril, and they will have watched the station and the Airport. They may have seen us get on the train. There is, in fact, every possibility of it."

"Oh, Carlos!" Marina expostulated. "I'm sure you're worrying unnecessarily. How could anyone have known? We go the back way out of the hotel; we travel in a baker's van to the station at such a speed that I'm sure no one could possibly have followed us. If these mysterious 'they' whoever they may be, were hanging about the station, they would certainly have missed the train. After all, we caught it only by a split second."

"How can we be sure?" Carlos almost exploded at her. "How can we be sure?"

"We can't," Marina said. "But we're here in a crowded express. Do you mean to suggest 'they' could possibly search every inch of it?"

"It's exactly what they would do," Carlos answered seriously. He saw the look of incredulity on

Marina's face and added: "Poor darling, you don't understand, do you?"

"I don't understand, and you're not helping me to," Marina answered. "Please, please, Carlos, start at the beginning and explain what all this is about. After all, I've trusted you; I've come with you, leaving all my clothes behind. That's a compliment which most women wouldn't be prepared to pay to anyone."

She gave a little laugh.

"It's ridiculous when you think of it, and two days ago I hadn't even met you."

She thought, as she spoke, of Sybil. What would she and all her friends say? They would think she was mad. Most of them, she was sure, would be suspicious of Carlos. "A new approach for a fortune hunter," she could hear them say!

She wondered for a moment wildly, if he was going to hold her up for ransom; and then she knew that, fantastic as it all seemed, her heart trusted him and she was prepared to stake her life on it that there was nothing phony about him. However extraordinary everything might appear to be, he himself was genuine enough.

Carlos turned suddenly and opened the door. He looked up the corridor and back the other way and came back into the room.

"I think I'll go and have a look round," he said.

"No!" Marina expostulated. "If things are as bad as you say they are, I'm not going to be left alone. Supposing you never came back? Supposing I waited and waited and then I had to go along the train and look for you. No. Please Carlos, stay with me."

He stood there hesitating, and she knew by the expression on his face that he was torn between what he thought he ought to do and her plea.

And then the door, which he'd not locked, opened almost silently. Carlos wheeled round with an expression of defiance on his face. Marina couldn't help it; she gave a little scream.

A man wearing a dark pull-on hat put his head round the door. He looked first at Carlos, then at Marina and, as neither of them spoke, he said in French:

"Pardon, Monsieur; pardon, Madame."

"What do you want?" Carlos asked in the same language in a furious tone.

The man opened the door a little wider.

"A thousand apologies," he said. There was no doubt that he was, in fact, a Frenchman. "I was just looking to see if this compartment was empty. On these trains the conductor always keeps a compartment or two up his sleeve for those who hand him a *pourboire*. I've learnt that it's wiser to confront him with an empty compartment than just to ask if he has one."

"I'm afraid this one's engaged," Marina said, evidently feeling there was nothing sinister in this and wondering why Carlos did not speak.

"So I see," the Frenchman answered. Then he added with a little smile, *"Bonne nuit, madame et monsieur."*

"Attendez, monsieur!"

The door had almost shut behind the visitor when Carlos spoke.

He moved forward and pulled the door open. The Frenchman's hand was still on the outside handle.

"Come in a moment, Monsieur. I have something to say to you."

"Indeed?" The Frenchman raised his eyebrows, but did as he was asked.

He took off his hat politely and Marina saw that

he had dark hair brushed back from a square fore-head. He was about the same height as Carlos and the two men faced each other warily.

"Madame and I have no use for this compartment," Carlos said slowly. "I suggest you take it on the condition that you do not say anything to the con-ductor. I wouldn't like him to think we had moved after all the trouble he has taken."

"But, Carlos!" Marina cried in astonishment. He did not seem to hear her.

"Is that agreed, *monsieur?*" he asked the French-man.

"*Mais, certainement,*" the Frenchman replied. "If you will permit me, I will get my—" he hesitated a moment, "—my friend."

"Of course," Carlos agreed. "We'll wait here until you return."

"Thank you, *Monsieur*, I am very grateful."

The Frenchman bowed to Carlos and to Marina and all smiles he left the compartment.

"Are you crazy?" Marina said almost angrily. "There's nothing wrong with this compartment, and we may not get another one."

"We're not going to get another one," Carlos replied.

"But why? Why?" Marina asked. "Surely you don't intend to sit up all night?"

"You must trust me," Carlos said. "I know I'm doing the right thing. I can't prove it to you, but I just know we mustn't stay here."

He had no time to say more.

The Frenchman's friend could not have been far away and now she appeared, a gorgeous apparition in pale mink, her hair dressed high on her head with diamonds sparkling in her ears.

The Frenchman was obviously proudly about to

introduce them, but Carlos put his hand under Marina's arm and yanked her to her feet.

"I hope you'll be very comfortable, *Monsieur,*' he said. "You will of course keep to our arrangement and not inform the conductor."

"There will be no need for us even to see him," the Frenchman replied reassuringly. "Anything we require we have brought with us."

He held out a large basket covered with a white cloth, out of which peeped all too obviously the golden cork of a bottle of champagne.

"We just don't want to be disturbed," the girl said with a provocative glance at Carlos.

"Then *bonne nuit, Monsieur et Madame,*" Carlos said with a mischievous imitation of the Frenchman's previous good-bye.

"And to you, also," the Frenchman replied, his eyes twinkling.

Carlos almost pushed Marina into the passage and shut the door behind them.

"I really think this is most unnecessary," Marina started to say.

Her words fell on deaf ears. Carlos was already striding ahead of her down the corridor, and there was nothing she could do but follow.

She noticed with dismay they were walking toward the back of the train, back past the second class coaches and on to the third.

Marina felt her heart sink as they reached the uncomfortable coaches where wooden seats, set on either side of the narrow aisle were filled with people of all nationalities and all classes.

There were fat, dark Portuguese women in their best black, the men in berets with handkerchiefs round their necks. There were students wearing climb-

74

ing boots and fantastic sweaters embroidered with the name of their favourite pop singer.

There were middle class business men who obviously thought it more thrifty to travel the cheapest way, and there was a number of cackling tourists who were "doing Europe" and for which they had doubtless saved the whole year.

The air was already heavy with smoke and there was the unmistakable smell of garlic.

One of the students was playing a mouth-organ and at the very end of the coach a couple of drunken sailors were singing extremely badly and out of tune.

Carlos stopped and said to Marina as she caught up with him: "Stand here a moment."

She wondered what he was about to do as he went to one packed seat and bent down to speak to an elderly man and woman who were sitting there with resigned faces, a part of their luggage packed around their feet.

"What can he be talking about!" Marina wondered. And then she saw Carlos take something from his pocket and pass it to the man and the man gave him something in return.

She swayed to the movement of the train, holding on to the top of the hard seat, conscious that there was a soldier on her right with his eyes on her in an inviting manner which she knew only too well.

The couple of whom Carlos had been speaking rose to their feet and collected their belongings—a bundle in a tartan rug, two baskets packed with what looked like food, a zipped bag bulging at the sides and finally from under the seat itself a small and very battered suit-case.

They pushed their way past the other passengers who stared at them resentfully. As they reached the aisle, the man spoke to Carlos:

75

"Thank you, Senhor."

He spoke in Portuguese and then they trudged past Marina through the connecting way into the next carriage.

Carlos with a smile on his lips indicated with his hand the seats they had vacated. Marina looked at him incredulously, but it was impossible to argue in the aisle of the coach or even to speak above the noise of the singing, the mouth-organ, the chatter of thirty or forty voices.

She stepped a little disdainfully between the knees of the two men on the outside and sat down on the seat next to the window.

"What have you done?" she asked in a whisper as Carlos sat down beside her. "Why have those people given us their seats?"

"I've given them our first class tickets," Carlos answered almost beneath his breath.

"Why?" Marina asked.

"I explained that my wife was very angry with me for having been so extravagant and I asked them to save me from a long journey on which I should be incessantly nagged. He was a sympathetic man. He understood my predicament."

Carlos's eyes twinkled; but Marina's lips tightened.

"You can't expect me to sit here all night," she whispered.

"I've been in worse places," Carlos answered. "It's unlikely anyone will look for us here."

Marina gave a sigh. It seemed incredible that Carlos had given up their comfortable sleeper and then their first class tickets for a third class seat with the smell, smoke and noise which, she thought resentfully, was likely to last the whole night through.

"I'm sorry, darling," Carlos said against her ear. "I love you, you know that."

His words seemed to make her heart turn over in her body. She wasn't, however, prepared to give in so easily, but merely answered:

"You've a very funny way of showing it."

"When I explain, you'll understand."

"I'm beginning to mistrust this explanation," Marina replied. "I believe the whole thing is a mad game."

"I wish it were," he answered seriously, and she knew that, to him at any rate, this was no game and there was no pretence about the danger.

It was really impossible to talk because the two men sitting opposite could hear everything they was said, and besides, she felt that Carlos wanted her to be silent.

She had known enough men in her life to be aware that nothing was more tiresome than a chattering woman, so she bit back the questions that trembled on her lips, the curiosity which seemed to get more intense every moment, and resolutely shut her eyes.

It was going to be impossible to sleep, she knew that; but at least she could keep some of the smoke from the foul pipes and cheap brands of cigarettes from making her eyes smart.

She turned over in her mind everything that had happened since that first eventful morning when she had met Carlos. "No one would believe me," she thought to herself, "if I told them the story of what had happened to date."

She thought of how scandalised and shocked Sybil would be at the idea of her running away from the hotel by a back exit, leaving all her clothes hanging up in the wardrobe and her personal possessions scattered about the room. She wondered what the management would make of it.

"At least they don't know anything about Mary

Marshall and aren't likely to find out who she really is. Never before have I left without paying my bill," Marina thought with a little smile.

She decided that when she got home she would send them a cheque for the right amount, with some explanation as to why Mary Marshall had been called away so hurriedly.

"When I get home."

The words which she thought in her mind seemed to be repeated again and again by the sound of the wheels. Would she ever get home?

Carlos was right. They were both in danger. What sort of danger and from whom?

Marina tried to think of all the things that Carlos might have done. Had he robbed a bank? But she was somehow certain it was nothing to do with money. Of course he had plenty, and that in itself was suspicious.

He had pulled a large wad of notes out of his pocket when he paid for the tickets; he left substantial tips wherever they went; he always ordered the best, most expensive wines, the dishes that were starred on every menu.

She thought of his clothes. They were plain and unobtrusive; they were the type of clothes any English gentleman might buy or a man who had been brought up in the Public School tradition—a plain grey suit, one that was well-cut by a first class tailor, expensive shirts, cuff-links of gold or platinum.

If it wasn't money that was the root of Carlos's trouble, what was it?

Could he, as he had jokingly said before, be a spy of some sort, in the pay of one country or another? Somehow it didn't seem possible. There were far too many books written about the excitements of the Secret Service or Interpol for anyone to take the thing seriously, or expect to meet a man battling against desperate odds with the enemy. But then, who were "they"?

She tried placing the nationality of the two men who had knocked on her bedroom door. Somehow she didn't think they were South Americans, which would be the obvious explanation. They were not French or Portuguese; they seemed almost stateless; men to whom one couldn't put a name.

The train was going faster and gradually the noise in the carriage was dying down. People were dozing uncomfortably against the hard backs of their seats.

One man had a handkerchief over his face. A woman had pulled a shawl over her head and around her face, so that only the tip of her nose was showing.

Marina stretched her feet a little further out in front of her. She was thankful she had slipped on a pair of comfortable sandals because by this time her legs would have been aching.

She opened her eyes and found Carlos was looking down at her.

"Are you comfortable?" he asked.

It was such a ridiculous question she couldn't help smiling.

"No comment," she replied.

He put his arm round her shoulders and drew her close.

"Put your head on my shoulder," he said. "It's correct in these circumstances. When in Rome, etc."

He looked across the aisle and saw there were three couples all comfortably snuggled against each other, the women using the men's shoulders.

"Of course it's correct," she whispered.

She felt a little thrill as his arm tightened and drew her even closer to him.

"It's not as romantic as it might have been," he said against her ear.

"Romantic is hardly the word I would have chosen for this journey," Marina smiled.

"You never know," he said; "it's in circumstances like these one gets to know one another better."

"Too well," Marina answered and then moved away. "I'm sure my nose is shiny."

She pulled her compact out of her bag. It was of gold with her initials inset in rubies and diamonds. She saw Carlos look at it and wondered why she had been such a fool as not to remember that it had cost a lot of money.

"It's not real," she lied quickly and realised as she said it that it was a stupid thing to have said.

"I wasn't born yesterday," he replied. "Who gave it to you?"

His eyes narrowed and she knew with a throb of her heart that he was jealous.

It is for every woman a moment of excitement when she becomes aware that the man who loves her is jealous of her. A little smile curved Marina's lips. She could see it in the tiny mirror of her vanity case as she touched up her mouth with lipstick.

"I also have my secrets," she answered, "Just as you have yours."

"If there weren't so many people around us I'd throw it out the window," Carlos said.

She looked up at him almost in alarm. She saw the fire in his eyes and the hard line of his lips.

She felt the excitement within her mounting. Could any man look like that and not love almost uncontrollably?

She put the vanity case carefully back into her bag and turned her face towards him.

"Do I look better?" she asked.

80

In answer he dragged her roughly back into the shelter of his arms.

"If you look at me like that," he muttered, "I shall kiss you."

For a moment their eyes met and it seemed to Marina as though there was a passage of arms between them, but it ended in her surrender.

She could not bear the intensity of the passion that she saw in his face, or the hungry desire of his lips. She felt herself quiver and because she was all too aware of the other passengers around them, she dropped her eyes beneath his and set her head back against his shoulder.

"I'm going to sleep," she said in a voice which trembled, but not from tiredness.

"I'll give you a new one when we get to Paris," Carlos said fiercely.

Again Marina wondered uneasily if he had robbed a bank and if it was his ill-gotten gains that he was spending on her.

After a while the tension of his arm around her relaxed; she knew that for a long time he had been watching her face; and because she dared not evoke that strange communication between them which had left her breathless, she kept her own eyes shut.

They must have travelled miles before finally she felt the tension go out of him and then there was something comforting, almost cosy in their closeness.

She could hear his heart beating. She could smell the very faint fragrance of expensive soap or, perhaps, aftershave lotion.

She felt contentment seep over her. Now no longer was she questioning, worrying, or going back over the past. She was content with the present. "Content". That was the right word, she told herself.

How extraordinary it was that Marina Martyn

should be content, sitting on the hard seat of a third class carriage with the arms of a man she had only known two days holding her close to him!

Some time later she felt Carlos stir and pull her coat over her legs.

It was still dark outside. At least she thought so. It was difficult to be sure because the heat, fog and smoke in the carriage had misted the windows.

She had opened her eyes sleepily as he moved. Now she closed them again and snuggled back against him. She thought he kissed her hair, but she wasn't sure. She was drifting between wakefulness and sleep and nothing was very clear.

Marina must have slept for some hours. She awoke with a jerk to hear the conductor asking for their tickets and their passports.

There was the usual flurry and commotion; people opening their cases, rummaging in their overcoats, searching in their pockets for the small pieces of pasteboard which had cost them so much money. And then everyone settled down again.

"What's the time?" Marina asked after she had put her passport back in her bag.

Carlos looked at his watch.

"A quarter to four," he said. "After all, if you were in London you might just be leaving the Duchess's ball."

"I never stay so late," Marina said. "And you?"

"I never get home 'till dawn when I'm gambling," he replied.

She smiled.

"And that's what you feel you're doing now?"

"I'm risking everything on the turn of a card," he replied.

"Everything?"

He nodded.

"Forget it and go to sleep," she admonished. "I've been to sleep; I have even forgotten the discomfort of this seat."

"My arm slept too," he said with a little smile.

"Oh, did I give you cramp? Why didn't you move?"

"I was watching you and thinking about you," he replied.

"And did you come to any special conclusion?" Marina enquired.

"Remind me to tell you all about it," Carlos said.

Two men appeared at the far end of the carriage. They may have been passengers, but to the trained eye they might have been officials. Marina wasn't sure.

Carlos turned towards her and hid his face in her hair.

"Go to sleep," he whispered. "If we keep talking people might notice."

Marina gave a sigh.

"So you're still worried, still feeling unsafe."

She wondered if perhaps he had persecution mania. She had heard of people who believed that enemies were always pursuing them and that they were in danger even from those they knew well.

It was a kind of neurosis that people laughed at, but it didn't seem to fit in at all with Carlos. You couldn't really imagine him being neurotic or hysterical or even imaginative to the point of being absurd.

She wanted to think about him. It was difficult while she could feel his face so close against hers. She shut her eyes and let the feelings he evoked sweep over her like waves.

This was not a repetition of the joys she had remembered feeling as a teenager. It was something far better. Far more wonderful, as she had known in that moment when he had kissed her on the battlement. . . .

She must have fallen asleep. When she awoke again it was to find daylight flooding the carriage.

Carlos looked at his watch.

"I'm going to wash," he said. "You'll be all right for a few minutes."

It seemed ridiculous to think she could be anything else. There was a fat, red-faced man opposite her who looked like a butcher, but who was very likely a prosperous commercial traveller. There was the woman who had sat next to Carlos counting the change in a worn purse. She must have gone to market a thousand times in search for good, cheap food for her family. The students were awake and playing "Yankee-Doodle-Dandy" on the mouth-organ.

It was all so ordinary, so commonplace. Everyone looked rather hot, shiny and dishevelled, their clothes creased and their hair untidy.

How could anyone imagine any sinister happenings in a scene like this?

Marina watched Carlos walk down the coach. There was something lithe and springy in the way he moved. She wondered if he was athletic and was quite certain he was.

How absurd it was that she knew so little about him. It didn't seem possible that one could say to a man one loved and in whose arms one had spent the night, "Do you like cricket?" or "Are you fond of golf?"

She knew without asking that he would be magnificent on a horse, not only because she knew it was characteristic of South Americans, but there was something about him which made her think of the open air, riding across great empty expanses of country.

She had a sudden longing to go riding herself over the green vales of England with the wind in her face and the sun on her uncovered head. How could she have been so silly as to have spent so much time in London, she thought.

Why didn't she take a house in the country, or better still a ranch in California or Texas, as one of her father's relations had once suggested she should do. She made excuses for not doing it; but she had given no one the real reason. She had been afraid of being lonely.

In London, Paris, New York there had been no chance of that. There had always been people; people who knew her; people who wished her to entertain them.

Marina sat up suddenly. How stupid she was! She hadn't thought of it before. When they got to Paris, there was every likelihood that she would meet someone she knew. It might be not only a matter of avoiding "them", but of not running into her own friends.

A little voice at the back of her mind asked, "Isn't it time you told him the truth?" and the answer came severely, "No, let him believe me to be no one. It's better that way."

She knew all too clearly why she thought it was better. Because she didn't want to see in his eyes that expression that was half admiration and half greed which she knew so well when people knew who she was—the fabulously rich Marina Martyn.

She had once said to a friend: "No one ever talks to me in a normal tone of voice. They have a particular tone in which all their conversations are couched, just because it is me and just because I'm rich."

"What nonsense!" her friend laughed. "You're imagining things."

But Marina knew she was speaking the truth.

People couldn't help it. They were brought up to admire those who had money without having to work for it. They couldn't help either envying her or hating her because she had so easily what they had to strive to attain.

"When we're in Paris we must avoid everyone I know," she thought resolutely and imagined that at least for the moment she was safe.

None of her friends would think in their wildest dreams that they would find Marina Martyn sitting crushed and dishevelled on a seat of a third class carriage.

She saw Carlos return, his eyes searching for her, a smile on his lips, and she felt that sudden leap of her heart which told her how much he meant to her. What did it matter if she was uncomfortable? He was there and for the moment at any rate they were together.

"We shall be in in half an hour," he said as he sat down beside her. "Are you hungry?"

Marina shook her head.

"Not particularly; but what I want more than anything else in the world at the moment is a bath."

"I'll have to see if I can find one," he said.

"It'll not be difficult in Paris," she said with a touch of irony.

The man who had been sitting opposite them and who had left the carriage some time ago returned. He sat down beside the red-faced man who looked like a butcher and said in French:

"There's a terrible commotion in the Sleeping Cars."

"What's happened?" the red-faced man asked.

"Well, I don't know exactly. The conductor on the next coach was telling me that two people got done in during the night."

"What d'you mean?" the red-faced man asked.

"Murder, the conductor thought it was," his friend

replied. "He hadn't seen it for himself, he hadn't had time to go along, but he had managed to get a message to the police to meet the train in Paris."

"I hope they don't delay us for long," the red-faced man said surlily. "I've got an appointment and I don't want to be late."

Carlos bent forward.

"Excuse me, M'sieur," he said in his fluent French, "did you say there had been a murder on the train?"

"That's right," the other man answered with relish, "a man and a woman. The conductor says nobody knows how it was done, but the conductor of this car says he didn't give them the compartment either."

Marina put out her hand and slipped it into Carlos's. She could feel the blood draining away from her face.

So it was true. Carlos hadn't been exaggerating. "They" had been looking for them and had struck blindly at the people who had taken their compartment. The Frenchman, who was not unlike Carlos when she came to think about it, and the girl in the mink coat had died.

She tried to imagine them lying dead, sprawled in their bunks, and somehow it didn't seem credible.

"It seems a grim thing to have happened," she heard Carlos say.

The man opposite shrugged his shoulders.

"Who knows," he said, "They may have killed each other. There are a lot of *crimes passionnés* these days."

"That's very true," the red-faced man said. "I hope this doesn't make me late for my appointment. I can't tell the police anything."

"I don't suppose anyone can," his companion agreed.

Carlos looked at his watch.

"We shan't be long now," he said to Marina.

He picked up a silk handerkerchief, put it over her head and tied it under her chin, and as he did so, he whispered:

"Keep with the crowd. Follow those students, if possible. Mingle with them. Whatever you do don't get detached."

She felt fear engulf her. She thought that until this moment she had never really believed in the danger of which Carlos had talked.

It was so easy to be swept away by another person's fear, another person's imagination. She had gone with him because he had been so insistent.

She thought she believed him, but one clear, critical part of her brain remained detached; had reiterated that all he had been telling her was a game, something that didn't happen in ordinary people's lives.

But those two people who had taken their sleeper were dead. The young Frenchman with his flashy friend. Had they had time to drink the champagne, Marina wondered, before they died?

Had they, perhaps, been asleep in each other's arms when death had come to them so unexpectedly, so unfairly?

She felt almost like accusing Carlos of contriving their death. After all, he had given them the sleeper on condition they did not tell the conductor.

For a moment she felt he too was a traitor, then she realised that was unfair. Carlos had given them his sleeper, but he could not have anticipated that their enemies would strike blindly in the dark without knowing whom they had killed.

They must have questioned the conductor as to whom he had given sleepers.

"A dark man with a young woman."

That might have pointed to thousands of people.

But there could only be one couple who had got on board with such haste at Lisbon: one couple who would have paid so much, perhaps too much for a compartment to themselves.

She could see all too clearly what had happened; and she only hoped the two people who had died in their place had died without knowing what was happening.

The train was drawing into the station. There was a whistle and a sudden darkening of the light as they ran under the protection of the station roof.

Now they could hear the voices of the porters: "*Porteur? Porteur?*" in their baggy blue blouses with their caps set at an angle as they crowded towards the first and second class coaches.

No one was worrying about the third class passengers who were picking up their own cases and starting to push into the aisle with the usual senseless anxiety to save a few seconds after hours of inaction.

Marina pushed herself in behind the students, Carlos's hand in hers. He was carrying her white vanity case and she realised it looked very out of place beside the knapsacks, canvas bags and parcels in which the students had stowed their belongings.

Now they were on the platform and the crowds were milling around.

"Move quickly. Don't look about you," Carlos whispered.

She tried to obey him, conscious of the tenseness of every muscle. There might be someone watching out for them.

She had a glimpse of *gendarmes*—half a dozen of them and two or three men in plain clothes—getting into the First Class Sleeper, the one that was second from the engine.

She didn't give them a second glance. She didn't

want to look. She only wanted to forget that two people had died instead of herself and Carlos.

Now they had reached the barrier, had given up their tickets and were through, pushing their way through the crowd of people watching the train indicator or struggling with heavy suit-cases towards the taxi rank.

Carlos, still holding her by the hand, pulled her first this way and then that until they were out of the station and onto the road.

"We're taking a 'bus," he announced but at that moment a small, dilapidated taxi appeared and he changed his mind.

It was going to turn into the station, but Carlos put out his hand. The taxi stopped. It was so small that they almost had to crawl into the seat at the back.

Carlos gave the driver an address which through the noise of the traffic Marina couldn't hear, and then they were off.

Carlos sank back against the seat, then he turned his head to look out of the rear window. There was much traffic and with the crowds going to and from the station it was impossible to know whether they were followed or not.

"D'you think it's all right?" Marina asked.

He frowned as if to warn her not to say anything that might in any way sound suspicious.

She had spoken in English, but then she remembered that most of the taxi drivers in Paris spoke at least a little English.

"Yes, I'm sure it's going to be all right," Carlos said. "You'll feel better after you've had some breakfast."

"I'm really not hungry now," Marina said, feeling as she spoke that it would be impossible for her ever to eat anything again.

She kept thinking of a bottle of champagne half hidden by a white cloth.

They drove in silence. The streets were busy in the early morning traffic, but the atmosphere of Paris was, Marina thought, as it had always been.

There was a smell about it, with the grey houses, the shutters, the bedding hanging from the upper windows, the trees along the boulevards, the children skipping along with their balloons on a string, which would have made Paris recognisable even if one had been led into it blindfold.

The sunshine glittered on the shop-windows and she had a sudden thought how wonderful it was to be in Paris with Carlos. She wondered if there would be a chance of their wandering hand in hand beside the Seine, staring at the pictures in the Louvre or sitting, as she had seen so many others sit, in the Tuilleries Gardens, oblivious of everything else.

She felt Carlos's hand touch hers and knew what it was she had always missed in Paris before.

Impulsively she turned towards him, forgetting the long, uncomfortable night, the murder of the people who had taken their place, the fear and worry of the future; forgetting everything except that she was in Paris and that Carlos was with her.

"Isn't it wonderful?" she asked, and her eyes were shining.

5

The taxi crossed the Seine and after driving through some narrow, ancient streets on the Left Bank it stopped outside a tall, rather dilapidated house which had a notice of lodgings to let in one of the windows.

Marina looked at the peeling paint and the cracked windows on the ground floor and then turned to Carlos with raised eyebrows.

"It's all right," he said in English. "I lodged here when I was at the Sorbonne."

He helped her out of the Taxi, paid the driver and with his hand under her arm hurried her through the double doors to a narrow, dark courtyard.

There were several doors leading off the courtyard, but Carlos went to the furthest one and here Marina saw again the shabbiness, the cracking paint and the general air of poverty which had characterised the outside of the building.

But Carlos was smiling as he rang the bell, and when, a few seconds later, the door was opened by a large fat woman with greying hair and wearing a white apron, he gave, to Marina's astonishment, a cry of sheer delight.

"Maman," he exclaimed, "you're just the same! I knew you would be. It's Carlos! Carlos! You remember me?"

The fat woman was as pleased to see Carlos as he

was to see her. She gave him a smacking kiss on each cheek and held him at arm's length exclaiming:

"*Voilà!* you've grown into a handsome man as I knew you would. Ah! *mon petit brave,* it's good to see you again!"

There was no doubting the sincerity of her welcome. Her whole big body seemed to quiver and shake with excitement and her dark eyes, framed in rolls of fat, twinkled and sparkled as she went on:

"All my nice boys come home in time—*mes petits fils,* as I call them. What woman ever had a larger or a better family? But if only you had let me know, the others would have been waiting here to greet you."

She led the way into the hall, still talking.

"You remember Lulu? She's married and has two children; Jacques, he's just the same, always coming into a fortune which never arrives!"

Her laughter rang out. She might, Marina thought, have been any mother greeting a son she loved, who had returned to her after only a short time away.

It was as if an effort Carlos remembered her presence.

"Maman," he said, "this is Marina."

"You wife?" the fat woman asked.

"No, no," Carlos replied, "my friend. She had been very helpful to me. We are travelling together."

"*Mais, oui,* I understand," was the answer and Marina thought, with a little smile that the Frenchwoman managed to convey in those few words so much more than was really necessary.

She held out her hand, but Maman would have none of it: she pulled Marina to her and kissed her cheek.

"Any friend of Carlos," she said, "is welcome in this house. Come into the kitchen, my dears. You'll want a meal if you have been travelling and it shall be ready for you just as quickly as I can cook it."

Marina hesitated, then said almost apologetically: "Would it be possible for me to have a bath?"

"*Mais, certainement*, nothing is easier," Maman exclaimed looking up the high stair which climbed out of the small, dingy hall, flight after flight to the top of the high house.

"You'll find the bathroom—" she began, and then she shrugged her shoulders. "Show her, Carlos, and light the geyser for her. You know how dangerous that one can be if it's not treated gently."

"D'you mean to say 'The Mule' is still with us?" Carlos asked.

"The very same," Maman replied; "and she still has a kick and will blow off your eyebrows if you're a little rough, yes?"

"Come on," Carlos said to Marina, "I'll show you how it works and I warn you, you'll either be roasted alive or frozen to death. There's no half measures with 'The Mule'."

"In ten minutes I will have a little meal ready," Maman said and waddled away to the kitchen as Carlos, taking Marina's vanity case in one hand and slipping his other arm through hers, led her up the stairway. It was so narrow, it was difficult for two to walk abreast.

Where in England there would have been a smell of damp and watery cabbage, instead, wafting up from the kitchen was a delicious aroma which made Marina feel hungry.

"I can't tell you what a wonderful person Maman is," Carlos said in his low, attractive voice. "She looked after all the students who lodged here exactly as if they were her sons. I think she thought of us in that way. Her children have been a trial to her. Lulu was always a prostitute. She has two children—although it's very doubtful who the fathers are. Jacques is just a crook who would milk his mother of every penny for some wild enterprise and would never appear again until he had lost the lot and his stomach was empty.

"She seemed very pleased to see you," Marina said.

"I loved her," Carlos answered. "I think the happiest time of my life was the months I spent at the Sorbonne. Academically, the result was pretty poor, but I learnt to speak French almost as well as a native and I learnt a great deal about life."

They reached a landing on the second floor and Carlos stopped.

"Here's the bathroom," he said. "It's certainly not been painted since I left."

It was a small, airless room with an ancient, stained bath fed by a geyser which looked as though it had been drawn by Fougasse.

"What about a towel?" Marina suggested.

"I'll get you one," Carlos answered, "as soon as I've got 'The Mule' going. Maman's linen cupboard is just down the passage. She always believes she keeps everything locked and nobody can get in; but there's a way of manoeuvring the handle, which we all knew, enabling us to filch a towel whenever anyone wanted one."

He spoke like a boy, and for a moment, Marina could see him clearly, running back eagerly from his classes, clattering up the stairs, sitting on the beds of the other students, discussing life with terrible intensity, as though their future hung on their words.

She wished she had known him before this dark cloud or whatever it was, had encroached upon him and left him worried and anxious with little lines already appearing on his forehead.

"Carlos," she said quickly, "tell me—"

Her words were lost in a sudden explosion as the gas of the geyser lit with a roar. Carlos jumped back as if to avoid the falling of a bomb.

"It's on!" he cried triumphantly above the noise.

A thin trickle of water was coming from the tap into the bath.

"It'll take about ten minutes," he shouted above the hissing. "I'll try and find you a room nearby where you can change."

He hurried out of the bathroom, opening the doors to right and left and then called:

"Marina, I've found one!"

She followed the direction of his voice and found him standing in a small, narrow room which contained an iron bedstead and a strip of carpet on the floor. The chest of drawers had lost a leg and was propped up with a brick.

"An empty room," Carlos told her. "You can change here and walk along to the bath in your overcoat."

Marina opened her mouth to say something, but shut it again.

"It's a bit primitive, I know," said Carlos almost as if he would be surprised if she had thought so; "but no one who ever stays here would exchange No. 5 Rue de Dupont for the Ritz Hotel."

He vanished before he finished speaking and came back with a small, quite inadequate, green towel.

"I've not forgotten how to work the lock!" he said proudly.

Marina took the towel from him with a smile. While he had been gone she had caught a glimpse of herself in a piece of broken mirror which was propped up on the mantelpiece. She had been appalled at what she saw.

Her face looked tired and her hair was untidy. She glanced down at her hands and saw they were begrimed with the dirt from the train, and her smart Dior suit had certainly not been improved by sitting up in it all night.

"Go away," she said to Carlos, "I'll join you downstairs as soon as I feel cleaner."

"All right," he answered. "Give me a shout if 'The Mule' misbehaves."

"If I'm still intact and capable of shouting, I'll do just that."

She shut the door behind her and started to undress.

It was well over half an hour later, when feeling a very different person, she walked down the stairs to the kitchen. Her hair was still a little damp, with the curls close to her head shining with little glints of fiery gold. Her face was clean and newly made-up, and although her skirt and blouse were still creased, she was conscious of feeling and looking her best.

She found the kitchen quite easily and discovered Carlos sitting at a table talking earnestly to Maman, who was slipping an omelette from the pan, so golden, so light and obviously so moist inside that it made Marina's mouth water even to look at it.

Carlos jumped to his feet and pulled out a chair for her.

"If you'd been a moment, later," he said. "I'd have begun without you. I've just warned Maman I could eat a horse."

"*Parlez français, Carlos,*" Maman admonished.

They both roared with laughter so that Marina guessed this was an old joke and the students at No. 5 Rue de Dupont were forced to speak French so that they could improve their vocabulary.

The omelette was delicious and so were the big

97

cups of steaming black coffee, the fresh French bread and great pats of yellow butter.

"What a difference food makes," Marina said with a little sigh. "I no longer feel frightened."

The door opened as she spoke and a young man with a small chin beard poked his head round the door. Maman gave a scream:

"Jacques!" she exclaimed. "Where have you been? Where have you come from?"

"Carlos, my old friend!" he exclaimed.

There was a great deal of hand-shaking and back slapping and Maman stood proudly by as if she had organised it especially for the benefit of both of them.

Marina was introduced and thought Jacques had a shifty expression and she personally wouldn't trust him with sixpence.

"You'll have something to eat, my son?" Maman enquired.

Jacques shook his head.

"No, I've eaten," he said, "but I'd like a drink if you have any decent wine in the house."

Maman fetched a bottle from the cupboard and he gulped down a couple of glasses of red wine, talking all the time to Carlos about his business ventures and how very nearly he had made himself a fortune.

"I'm on to something very good now," he said. "It's an invention of a friend of mine and we're going to share in the profits."

"What is it?" Carlos asked.

"It's a silencer which can be fitted to almost any aeroplane," Jacques answered.

"But they've been working on that for ages," Marina interposed, "but none of the airlines has come up with any solution so far."

"I think I have," Jacques asserted in a knowing way.

When he had finished his glass of wine, Jacques looked uneasily at his mother.

"Anyone in trouble in the house?" he asked.

"No one that I know of," she answered. "Why d'you ask?"

"There were a couple of chaps in the courtyard I don't like the look of," Jacques replied. "They were asking questions at the Bergare's house as I passed them. I thought they might be coming on here."

"A couple of chaps!" Marina caught her breath as she saw the expression in Carlos's eyes.

He jumped to his feet and asked quickly:

"What did they look like?"

"Foreigners of a sort; they were definitely not Frenchmen; that is the only thing I know."

"Fool that I am!" Carlos said. "I might have guessed they would expect me to come here. They would know this is where I stayed when I lived in Paris."

Marina felt the fear that had been with them all through the night come creeping up again to enfold them both in its deadly embrace so that her voice quivered a little as she asked:

"What shall we do?"

"Maman," Carlos said urgently, "is there another way out. I've forgotten. I never had to hide in those days."

Maman shook her head.

"Only through the front door, *mon brave*," she said, "except across the roof."

"The roof." Carlos repeated the word with a sudden lilt in his voice. "The others used to talk about it. I never used it. Show me, please show me, Jacques."

Maman, leaning heavily on the table, said to her son:

"Take Carlos and his girl friend out of here over

the roofs. You know the way, you've used it often enough."

Jacques seemed to sit back a little more comfortably in his seat.

"I'm tired," he said. "Why should I move?"

"Because I'll pay you," Carlos said and his voice was like ice. "That's what you're waiting for, isn't it? Come on, one hundred new francs to get us on the roof and one hundred more to take us down on the other side."

"Three hundred," Jacques said almost automatically, as though he felt forced to bargain even though the price was quite good enough as it was.

"Three hundred," Carlos said, "and count it as Maman's contribution towards your damned invention."

Jacques gave him a little twisted smile and got to his feet.

"Come on," he said. "They may be knocking on the door at any minute now."

Maman started to collect the dishes and cups hastily and stack them in the sink. Marina with a newly awakened perceptiveness realised that she was doing this to cover their tracks. It was something Maman had had to do in the past, she thought. There was no need to tell her it was necessary when people came asking questions.

Carlos, in one stride, reached her side. She had already put the coffee cups into the soapy water.

"*Merci Maman*," he said: "*merci mille fois*. I love you, you old angel."

He gave her a kiss, managed to pick up Marina's vanity case as he did so and at the same time slipped her coat over his arm.

"Come on," Jacques said and jerked his head towards the stairs.

100

With the words Jacques went ahead of them, moving almost silently so that he made Marina think of a cat.

They had reached the second floor and Marina was just about to make some remark about the bathroom to Carlos, when they heard the heavy clang of the doorbell.

"Only just in time," Carlos muttered.

Marina knew instinctively by the way the bell was pulled that it was no ordinary caller—no student in search of rooms or a tradesman delivering goods could have made the sound so unpleasant and authoritative.

They plunged up the next two flights and as they reached the top they heard the bell ring again and realised Maman was giving them plenty of time before she condescended to answer its summons.

On the top floor was a narrow ladder leading to a skylight. Jacques went up first, opened the skylight and then helped Marina out onto the roof.

As she stepped out a little gingerly she could not help giving a gasp, for below them was the Seine, blue and silver; and on the other side of the river the grey perfection of Notre Dame. There were barges passing along the river, but Carlos gave her no time to appreciate the scene.

He shut the skylight carefully behind them and said sharply:

"Follow Jacques; we have no time to waste."

The roof was gabled; many of the slates were off and the lead had cracked in the sun, so that Marina had to watch every step in case her heel caught in the jagged pieces. The roofs of the houses were all interlocked, so that it was difficult to know where one ended and another began.

It seemed to Marina that they walked for quite a long time before they came to a fire escape leading down perhaps one floor to a balcony and then on the other side another fire escape going down a little further.

She had always been rather afraid of heights and she dreaded the moment when they must descend, feeling she might make a fool of herself; but fortunately the fire escapes were so intricate, weaving in between house and house, across a flat roof here, a balcony there, that when finally a rusting ladder led them down into a small dirty yard she was quite surprised to find herself on the ground.

The yard was at the back of a timber merchant's; it was filled with piles of wood, and the sound of a saw came through an open door.

Jacques led them quickly towards a gate which obviously opened to the street outside.

"Wait a minute," Carlos said before Jacques could open the gate. "I want a car. Have you any idea where I can get one?"

"I've got a friend who will drive you anywhere you want to go," Jacques answered, "—at a price of course."

"Is he far from here?" Carlos enquired.

"About three minutes' walk."

"Then go and fetch him," Carlos commanded: "we'll wait here."

He saw Jacques hesitate.

"Tell him I'll pay him and there should be something in it for you."

Jacques seemed quite unabashed by the scorn in Carlos's voice; and then, as the Frenchman still seemed undecided, Carlos drew his notecase from his pocket.

"Afraid you can't trust me?" he asked. "You never used to be so suspicious."

He drew three hundred-franc notes from his wallet and held them out. Jacques almost snatched them and slipped them inside his pocket.

"Wait here," he said in a very different tone. "If Henri's there, I'll be back in a few minutes."

"If not, come and tell us," Carlos commanded.

Through the half open gate they saw Jacques sprint away, moving across the road at quite a decent pace.

"What a nasty young man!" Marina exclaimed.

"I've always disliked him," Carlos agreed. "He treats his mother abominably, but she loves him and is even grateful for the times he comes crawling home just because he's broke."

"Well, he's got a bit to be going on with now anyway," Marina said.

"And at this moment he'll be bargaining with his friend so as to make a bit more," Carlos said.

"D'you really think those men Jacques told us about were after us? How could they have known unless they had followed us from the station. I should have said that was impossible."

"You don't understand," Carlos answered. "It's far more complicated than that."

"Then tell me," Marina begged.

"What, here? he asked, making a gesture with his hands. He looked over his shoulder towards the carpenter's shop.

"I'll tell you everything the moment I can, darling. You know that, don't you?"

He looked down at her small, serious face and added involuntarily:

"God, I'm a brute to have done this to you, aren't I? You're so small and exquisite, fragile and lovely. I want to pick you up in my arms and carry you off somewhere safe, comfortable and luxurious."

His words made the colour come flooding to her face, and the expression in his eyes made her almost forget the danger they were in.

She forced herself to try and think calmly.

"Isn't there anyone who can appeal to?" she asked. "Suppose we went to some private person and told them what was happening?"

"That wouldn't help," Carlos answered. "We should only involve them as I've involved you."

"But . . ." Marina began, trying desperately to think of someone important and influential she knew in Paris.

The houses of the great bankers, politicians, the aristocracy where she had been an honoured guest. She knew so many people and yet, somehow, she couldn't see herself arriving with Carlos and asking them for sanctuary.

"There must be someone," she said desperately.

Carlos shook his head.

"We've got to rely on ourselves," he said. "In case I don't have the chance to say it again, I love you. I think you're magnificent—and I want to kiss you more than I've ever wanted anything in my life before."

It was impossible to think coherently when he talked like that.

The yard was dark and full of shadows and the sunshine could not reach the end, yet she felt they were standing together on top of the world.

She lifted up her face to his. She thought never had anything been so wonderful, so utterly dazzling as the happiness he gave her as their lips clung together.

Then there was the sound of a car outside and the hoot of a horn. Jacques flung open the gate.

"Come on," he said. "Henri says he can drive you for two hours and then he has got to get back. He has an engagement this afternoon."

"Thank you, Jacques—and be good to your mother."

Carlos looked at the small *Peugeot* standing outside and said sharply to Marina:

"Keep your head down and hurry: don't look about the street."

She obeyed him without question and when he had helped her in he jumped in after her. The car moved off.

"Where d'you want to go?" Henri asked.

He was a dark, thick-set young man who looked as though he came from the Basque country.

"South," Carlos answered: "and keep to the main roads."

Marina raised her eyebrows at this. She would have thought it would have been wiser to go by a less obvious route, and then she remembered that "they" might have fast cars and it was easier to be stopped in a lonely lane than on the broad highway.

She wished she had had time to discuss with Carlos where they should go, feeling that perhaps it would be safer in England than anywhere else.

But the body was still thrilling from his kiss and her lips felt warm and sensitive from the touch of his lips and she knew, if she was honest with herself, that it didn't matter where they went so long as they went together.

She felt, as they drove through the streets of Paris, that this was a mad dream from which it would be impossible to wake.

How could she, who had always stayed at the Ritz or with friends off the Champs-Elysées, who had lunched and dined at all the expensive restaurants and gone to all the most important parties, be creeping like a criminal out of Paris, to some unknown destination, driven in a rickety car which smelt of cheap petrol by a young man who obviously had a penchant for garlic?

"Where shall we get to in two hours?" she asked.

"I was just wondering that myself," Carlos answered. "Got a map on you?" he enquired of Henri.

The youth nodded towards the compartment filled with old plugs and dirty rags.

"You may find one in there," he answered laconically.

Carlos leant across the front seat and extracted some torn and filthy pieces of a map and tried to piece them together.

"Why don't we go to England?" Marina asked beneath her breath.

"How are we going to get there?" Carlos enquired. "I expect they will have thought of that, you being English."

"How should they know about me?" she asked.

"They're not fools," he answered beneath his breath.

"Why? Why? Why?" The words seemed to be written in front of Marina's eyes in scarlet and gold.

As Carlos pored over the map in the bumpy car, she tried to think back, to find some clue, some explanation as to where they had gone wrong in the first place, or how they could have avoided being hounded as they were being hounded now from pillar to post.

Had there really been two men in the courtyard of No. 5 Rue de Dupont? or had Jacques made it up? She remembered how she had doubted Carlos last night as she sat on the hard seat of the third class carriage and thought of the comfort of the sleeping car which he had given up to the middle aged gentleman and his *chère amie*.

It just couldn't be true that those two people were lying dead, and yet she had to force herself to accept it—"Why? Why? Why?"

Questions crowded in on her, and yet all the time she was conscious of Carlos beside her, with his hands strong and virile, yet beautifully manicured, holding the dirty map; with his clear-cut profile silhouetted against the window. His dark hair was brushed back from his forehead and she had an almost uncontrollable impulse to touch it.

"I love him," she thought.

Suddenly her millions were supremely unimportant and she knew all the money she had squandered in the whole of her life had never brought her one atom of happiness so poignant or so real as this.

She put out her hand a little timidly and touched Carlos on the knee.

"What's the verdict?" she asked in English.

"I don't know: I just don't know," he answered. "You see, they'll guess we'll do something like this: it's obvious, isn't it? They know that we know they were looking for us in Paris. Therefore, we get out of Paris. They know that it might be safer if we went to England, but we have got to get there. They'll be watching the railway stations and the airport. What possible alternative is there?"

"But how many of them are there?" Marina asked, only to get a frown from Carlos and a nod of the head in the direction of Henri.

"I'm sure he can't speak English," she whispered, knowing her voice was drowned by the noise of the engine.

"One can never be certain," Carlos answered.

"In which case," she thought helplessly, "there was no point in trying to talk about anything." One almost seemed to come back to the insurmountable fact that she didn't know what was happening and if things went on like this and she was never alone with Carlos it was unlikely she would ever learn.

"Were they police?" The same question as she had asked before; yet police were not likely to go about killing people in sleeping berths. Then in what sort of danger was Carlos involved?

She thought about it until her head hurt and yet she was not sure that it wasn't the rattle and discomfort of the car which was affecting her. There wasn't room for their legs at the back and the stuffing, if there ever had been any, had long since gone from the seat.

Henri drove well but very fast. He was obviously determined to get as many miles into the two hours as possible.

"By the way," Carlos said after some time, "what arrangements did Jacques make with you?"

"He told me you would pay me ten francs a kilometre," Henri replied.

"He did, did he," Carlos said grimly.

"No question about it, is there?" Henri asked, his foot moving from the accelerator towards the brake.

"No, of course not," Carlos said. "I was just making sure he had carried out my instructions."

He gave Marina a little wink as he spoke; she couldn't help smiling back—the crookery of that crafty Jacques!

It was quite clear that Henri wouldn't keep the ten francs a mile all for himself.

"And of course, there's the return journey," Henri said almost fiercely.

"Of course," Carlos answered. "Don't worry, we're very grateful to you, my friend."

The car seemed to gather more speed and though occasionally Marina held her breath, there was no doubt that Henri was an expert driver.

They passed through Fontainebleau and were soon heading down the road which led to the Côte d'Azur. Marina had travelled along it more than once either in a Rolls-Royce or a big Mercedes she often hired when she was in France.

She could recognise the little villages as they flashed through them. The grey chateaux standing in their walled gardens and sometimes a fountain playing in the spring sunshine.

"Are you tired?" Carlos asked her after they had been travelling over an hour.

"No," she replied. "One never seems to feel tired in France."

Even as she spoke she knew she had made a slip of the tongue. She had never hinted before ever having been in France, and now she wondered how soon it would be before he began questioning her, asking her where she had stayed or whom she had been with when she came to Paris.

To cover her confusion she opened her bag and took out her vanity case: she had it open before she remembered how much it had annoyed Carlos the night before. Now she saw him frowning at it.

"Did he love you very much?" he asked.

She didn't attempt to misunderstand him.

"No," she answered, "you needn't be jealous, honestly you needn't."

"You lied to me saying it was imitation," Carlos said accusingly.

"You frightened me," Marina admitted. "I didn't want you to come to silly conclusions: the person who gave me this wasn't in the least important the way you are thinking about it."

"You didn't love him?"

"Not in the least," she answered. "I wasn't even very pleased with it—and that's the truth."

She remembered with a little inward smile, how cross she had been when the bill came because it was more than she had expected. They had made some small alteration to the case and had charged exorbitantly because she was Marina Martyn. That sort of thing annoyed her, and she seldom used the case without thinking with resentment how she had been done.

"One good thing," she said quickly, "we can always sell it if we get hard up. We may need money before the end of this trip."

"There's always that possibility," Carlos agreed.

"We're certainly spending like drunken sailors at the moment," Marina said. "You could have hired a really good car for what this is costing us."

"And that's just what they might be looking for," Carlos answered.

Marina put her vanity case back in her bag with a little snap. She was getting fed up with "they". The conversation always seemed to end in the same way. It was like a very bad film, the faces coming out of the darkness and things happening you couldn't quite see, so that you never knew on whose side the people were, or exactly what was happening.

"In another ten minutes I shall have to turn back," Henri said. "I wouldn't go if it wasn't that it's the owner of the car I've got a date with."

"So it's not your's," Carlos said.

"No, I drive it for him," Henri replied.

"Let's hope he doesn't read the speedometer," Carlos said in an amused voice.

"It's broke," Henri answered.

They were passing through a flat piece of country. There were plenty of cars on the highway. Carlos looked over his shoulder. There were cars following them most of which flashed by the little Peugeot with contempt.

"Oh, look! There's a circus," Marina exclaimed
110

pointing to where on the outskirts of a village were the big tent, the caravans and the merry-go-rounds all set out on a flat field. The villagers were streaming towards them and a great banner was flying over the entrance announcing "Ted Johnson's Cowboy Circus".

"It's English!" she cried. "I seem to have heard of them."

"Stop!"

The small car was almost past the circus into the village as Carlos said the word. Marina turned her head and looked at him in surprise.

"Here?" she asked.

"Yes, here," he answered.

Henri put on the brakes and the car drew to a standstill.

"Drive round the back of the circus and drop us on the other side," Carlos commanded. "I don't want to get out in the road."

"All right," Henri agreed. "I hope I don't get stuck."

"The ground looks hard enough," Carlos answered, "and if you do, there's plenty of people to push."

They bumped over the rough entrance to the field where the circus was camped. They drove round the outside, bumping violently over the rough, tufty grass, till finally they were at the other side of the big tent where the ring of animal cages, caravans and lorries made a barrier through which the public couldn't pass.

"You can stop here," Carlos said, "and I'll pay you."

He took his wallet from his pocket.

"How many kilometres?" he asked, and when Henri told him, he said, "that's about ten more than

111

I make it, but as there's no one here to act as arbitrator, shall we split the difference?"

"That's all right," Henri answered.

Marina guessed that even with the deduction he was well in hand.

Carlos counted over some notes.

"Thank you very much," he said. "We're very grateful to you."

"That's all right, monsieur," Henri said and, showing some good manners for the first time, added: "*Au revoir, Monsieur; au revoir, Madame.*"

"*Au revoir*, Henri," Marina said.

With an effort she shook hands with him as it seemed to be expected of her. His hand was hard and extremely dirty: when he was out of sight she bent down and wiped hers on a tuft of grass.

"Now then," she said, looking up at Carlos, "what do we do now? Have fun on the merry-go-round?"

"I've got an idea," he answered. "First of all I want to park you somewhere where you'll be safe."

"You're not going to leave me?" she asked.

"Only while I have a talk with the Proprietor of the Circus," he answered.

"What are you going to do? Make him a take-over offer?" Marina asked with an effort at humour, but Carlos didn't seem amused.

"Come on," he said.

Walking cautiously round the circle of the circus, they found a side entrance through which a man was leading a horse.

"You can't come in here," he said in a rough voice. "The entrance for the public is round the front."

"I know that," Carlos answered, "but I want to see the boss."

He had asked the man in English and to Marina's surprise the answer came back in the same language.

The man was thin and dark and wiry with dark eyes. Marina had almost automatically expected him to be a foreigner. Now she realised he was, in fact, a Romany gypsy.

"What d'you want the boss for?" the gypsy asked.

"Thought he might have a job going," Carlos answered.

The gypsy looked him over more aggressively.

"What can you do?" he asked.

"Anything with horses, for one thing," Carlos replied.

" 'E's short of a groom," the gypsy volunteered.

"Thank you," Carlos said with a smile. "What's the boss's name?—Johnson?"

The gypsy nodded his head.

"Yes, Johnson's the name. You'll find him in the caravan painted red and white along there." He jerked his thumb.

"Thank you," Carlos said. "I'm very grateful."

"I don't suppose you'll get it," the gypsy said. " 'E's particular who 'e takes on."

He pulled on the bridle of the horse and started to walk away, then added:

" 'E don't like 'dolls' either."

"What's he mean by that?" Marina asked.

"I think we'd better say we're married," Carlos replied. "It seems that Mr Johnson is respectable."

"I don't know what you're talking about," Marina gasped. "Listen, Carlos, this is crazy!"

"Trust your uncle," he answered and without waiting further argument turned in the direction in which the gypsy had pointed, and Marina found herself hurrying behind him towards the red and white caravan.

"It's mad," she whispered under her breath; "completely and absolutely mad; and oh, God, I love him!"

113

6

The man sitting in the caravan was old with iron grey hair and a heavy, somewhat debauched face.

Marina guessed he had gypsy blood in him somewhere; but he might in other surroundings have easily been a prosperous stockbroker or head of a chain of stores. He had an autocratic bearing and an air of ruthlessness which showed all too clearly that he was used to power and to giving orders to others.

The very manner in which he looked Carlos up and down would have been offensive if one had not recognised that this man expected to be treated like a king.

"What do you want?"

Alfred Johnson spoke in English, and then added somewhat belatedly:

"You speak English?"

"Yes, sir."

Carlos's reply was respectful. When he went on talking Marina noticed with admiration the common accent that he affected, the roughness of his tones which disguised very effectively his usually cultured and educated voice.

Without waiting for Johnson to ask another question, Carlos said:

"I understand, sir, you're short of a groom. I'd like to apply for the position."

"Who told you that?" Alfred Johnson snapped, and

114

then as he obviously didn't expect an answer to his question continued: "D'you know anything about horses?"

"I was born and bred with them, sir."

"They all say that," Alfred Johnson retorted. "What experience have you had?"

"I've worked on a cattle-ranch in South America; I've trained racehorses; I rode before I could walk and I appreciate decent horseflesh," Carlos replied.

"It sounds glib enough," Johnson sneered. "Any references?"

"The ones I had were written in Spanish and Portuguese," Carlos answered; "I didn't bring them because I didn't think anyone would understand them."

"Damn your eyes, I can speak enough Spanish to take my Circus to Spain," Alfred Johnson answered; "and who's this?"

"This is my wife, sir."

"Wife, eh?" Johnson's eyes narrowed. "Have you got your marriage lines? I don't care for fancy pieces in my circus."

Marina felt the blood rise in her cheeks. How dare any man speak of her in that fashion? Carlos appeared quite unperturbed.

"I'll produce them for you if you'd like to see them, sir," he said with servility. "As a matter of fact, they're in Paris. We were married there only ten days ago. We're still on our honeymoon."

"Ten days, eh?" said old Johnson looking over Marina in a way that made her want to scream. "You haven't got round to buying 'your wife' a wedding ring."

It was the accent on "your wife" which made Marina long to strike him.

"Since you mention it, sir," Carlos said apologeti-

115

cally, "my wife had a ring, but we were obliged to pawn it. We've rather overspent ourselves, that's why we're looking for a job."

"So that's the explanation," Alfred Johnson said. "Well, I don't particularly want any more women round the circus—they're a damned nuisance."

"You'll find my wife is useful," Carlos said. "She sews very well; she was apprenticed to a dressmaker before I married her. She'd be prepared to mend and repair the clothes of the performers, as long as she could do it in our own quarters."

Marina took a deep breath. Really this was going too far. What did Carlos hope to gain by such a masquerade? She glanced at him, striving to catch his attention; but his eyes were fixed on the big, bulky figure of Alfred Johnson. There was just the right expression of eagerness and anxiety in his eyes as though he was in actual fact a man desperately in need of a job.

There was a long pause; then gruffly, and it seemed the decision was forced from him rather than that he made it willingly, Alfred Johnson said:

"Very well then; ninety francs a week and keep yourselves, that is, if you really can handle horses."

"Give me the most fiery-spirited animal you've got—one that's unbroken if possible—and I'll show you how I can ride it."

"No!" Alfred Johnson retorted. "You're to be a groom, not a damned circus performer. If I catch you cheating me over the food, or if the horses don't look their best, I'll kick you from here to Paris. Is that clear?"

"Absolutely clear, sir."

"Very well then. What're you waiting for?"

"I was just wondering where we could live," Carlos

116

answered. "We haven't got a caravan of our own or the money to buy one."

"I could be quite certain of that," Alfred Johnson retorted sourly. "I not only hire men, but they expect me to house them, and if I'm not bloody careful, I'll be feeding them as well. All right. There's an empty caravan as it happens, but you pay me twenty-five francs a week for it and do the repairs it needs out of your own pocket. Is that clear?"

"Yes, sir, thank you."

Alfred Johnson raised his voice.

"Luke, where the devil are you, boy?"

"Coming."

A boy of about sixteen came running across the trampled grass from another caravan. He had long dark hair, impudent black eyes, high cheekbones and a dark skin. Marina knew he was a Romany gypsy.

He gave them a friendly smile, then almost in the identical respectful tone that Carlos had used said to Alfred Johnson:

"Want me, Guv?"

"Yes," the circus proprietor replied. "Take this couple—they say they're married—to Mario's caravan, and then show the man where the horses are."

He turned away and as they were about to go asked harshly:

"You haven't told me your name."

"Carlos Ayelo," Carlos answered.

"Right. Don't be long getting to work."

They were dismissed and Luke was beckoning them down the long line of caravans and shouting above the music of the roundabouts.

"This way! I'll show you the caravan."

He walked ahead of them, his bare legs showing beneath a torn and patched pair of jeans, the sleeves of his T-shirt rolled up to show strong brown arms that were somehow in striking contrast to the too thin lines of his slender body.

"He hasn't been fed properly," Marina thought and was surprised at herself for noticing such a thing; for she was not particularly concerned with Luke, the Circus or the Fun Fair.

As they passed by it all she was thinking with indignation of the position in which they now found themselves. Surely this sort of masquerade was unnecessary? They could have stayed in the village or perhaps taken the train to some other destination. Why the Circus? And what on earth did Carlos expect to gain from it? On top of it all, that pretending they were married. She felt she didn't like the glib way in which the lie had come to his lips.

"I'm not going to stay here," she decided just as Luke reached a shabby caravan badly in need of paint, and opened the door.

It was a modern, streamlined caravan which must once have been expensive, but when Marina entered first the small kitchen with its stainless steel sink and then the main part of the van, she felt nearly sick at the dirt and dilapidation of it.

The floor was filthy. It was obvious that the last occupant had dragged up the carpet before he departed and the dust of months, or perhaps years, had collected under it.

The windows were dirty and some of the panes were cracked. The ceiling was peeling in large strips. There were two beds, both of which were convertible into seats or sofas in the day time; but mattresses and cushions had been removed with the exception of one which sprawled drunkenly on to the floor, its wadding sticking out as if it had been disembowelled by some savage hand.

"We can't stay here." The words had already

formed themselves on Marina's lips when she heard Carlos say:

"This'll do; it's nothing soap and water and scrubbing won't alter—with the exception of the mattresses. Where can I get new ones?"

Luke kicked the one on the floor.

"Not good enough for you?" he said. "Well, I don't blame you. You'll find that Ma Johnson has some new ones tucked away somewhere. She'll charge you for them—more than they are worth. There's no other way of sleeping comfortable—not till we get to Amiens at any rate."

"Where's her caravan?" Carlos enquired.

"Next to the Old Man's," Luke answered. "She has all the stores. You'll be able to get a bucket from her and some soap, if that's what you've got in mind."

He looked round the caravan.

"Mario always was a dirty beggar," he said. "He drank too much."

"What did he do?" Carlos asked.

"Acrobat," Luke replied. "He fell off the trapeze at our last stop. I think 'e broke 'is back."

There was something in the casual way in which Luke spoke which made her sorry for the unfortunate Mario.

"Bad luck," Carlos said.

"Bad judgment," Luke smiled. " 'Sides he was too old. You've got to be young in this game. Are you ready to see the 'orses?"

"Yes, I'll come with you now," Carlos answered. He turned to Marina:

"Wait here," he said, "I won't be long."

He was gone before she could answer him.

Through the small dirty window she watched him walk away with Luke towards the big tent of the Circus. His expensive suit was out of keeping and yet somehow Carlos was walking differently, less stiffly with the easy, swaying walk of a man who is used to riding. As she watched him, she saw him pull off his tie and tuck it into his pocket.

She tried to open the window to let in some fresh air. It was impossible and so instead she managed to force open the central door of the caravan which led directly into the main room.

The place smelt, the dirt was indescribable. "Nothing that some soap and water wouldn't alter," she heard Carlos saying; and now she wondered who he expected to scrub the floor, the walls and ceiling for that matter and Heaven knows! she wouldn't sleep on the beds even with a new mattress, unless they were scrubbed down too. Did he really expect her to do it?

She felt a sudden anger rise within her. It was her own fault! she was prepared to admit it. She shouldn't have gone with Carlos in the first place. She should have insisted on going down in the hotel and having an interview with the Manager, demanding that she be protected from the men who were asking to see her passport. Instead they had run away.

Even as she looked back she remembered what had happened during the train journey. The death of those two people, the girl with her mink coat, her tawdry jewellery; the man smirking happily over his bottle of champagne: and now, because Carlos was frightened, they were hiding here in the Circus!

She had not liked Alfred Johnson. He was obviously a hard, disagreeable man who would be prepared to chuck them out at the first hint of trouble, and yet somehow it was comforting that he spoke the same language. These were English people, her people.

If the worst came to the worst, she could appeal to

them; but would there be a chance of appeal? Wouldn't the men who threatened Carlos and perhaps her too strike first and talk after?

"There must be something we can do besides this," Marina thought.

She opened her bag and looked in her note-case. There was a big book of Travellers Cheques. Perhaps £250 worth. Sybil wouldn't have let her go abroad with less. There was a number of Portuguese notes and also some English ones.

"That's a comfort, at any rate," she thought. "There's enough to get rid of the filth of Mario's leavings."

She opened the door of a cupboard and found herself looking at her own reflection in the mirror that was fixed to the wall.

For a moment she found it hard to recognise the arrogant and sophisticated Marina Martyn. Her handkerchief was pulled tightly over her hair. Her nose was shiny. She had forgotten in all the excitement to put any lip-salve on her lips. Her face was strained both with fatigue and with anxiety.

She looked at her once smart, expensive suit; it had certainly not been improved by scrambling over dirty roofs. Her hands were filthy too. And without knowing it she must have touched her white blouse.

Marina stood staring at herself incredulously, and then she remembered that Carlos had seen her like this. What must he have thought?

She pulled the handkerchief from her head, combed her hair into place, thankful that she had washed it during the short time they had been at the Rue de Dupont. She powdered her nose, put on her lipstick and felt a little better. Still she was ashamed of her hands and went into the dirty, untidy kitchen wondering if there was any chance of water.

She turned on the taps and heard the gurgle which told her the water tank, wherever it might be, was empty.

Somehow, this was the last straw. No water!

The whole thing was ridiculous. Carlos must think of a better idea. "We'll go back to Paris," Marina decided. "We'll go to the Embassy—I'll explain to the Ambassador exactly what has happened."

Even as she made the decision she had the uncomfortable feeling that the Ambassador, whom she knew quite well, would say:

"Of course, my dear Marina, we will protect you and if you like, you can have half-a-dozen policemen or detectives to take you back to London; but your friend is a South American, why doesn't he go to his own Embassy?"

Diplomatic protocol loomed ahead like an almost insurmountable wall. Marina could see all too clearly how the British Embassy would meet any issue which they felt would interfere with diplomatic relations. All the same, there must be other places, Marina thought.

She remembered two or three names—international financiers, bankers, Statesmen, whom she knew personally. They surely, would help her. In the meantime all this nonsense had got to stop.

A slight wind slammed the caravan door and instantly she was conscious of the smell of dirt. She pulled the door open again angrily and as she did so saw Carlos coming back towards the caravan. He was carrying a mattress done up in cellophane on his back, and Luke was carrying another.

Carlos was in his shirt sleeves. He had taken off his coat and had hung it through a belt which he wore round his waist. He was laughing at something he had said to Luke and somehow, at that moment, Marina felt alone and unwanted.

Already he seemed to have adapted himself to the circus life and to the lies he had told to enact the character he had created out of his imagination. In that split second she saw herself fighting against him though he didn't even know it, watching and criticising, determined not to make the best of this almost impossible situation.

It was then that behind Luke she saw a gypsy child with long hair, a tattered dress, carrying over her bony little arm a large new galvanised bucket.

"He means it," Marina thought." He means me to scrub out this pigsty. I won't do it! I'm going—I'm going home."

She slammed the door of the van determined not to speak to Carlos in front of Luke and the child. She heard them go to the other end of the caravan, heard Carlos's voice, light and amused, say:

"Put the mattresses down on the grass—we don't want them dirtied before we have to use them. And thank you, Lena, for bringing the bucket. I'll spend my first week's wages buying you a bag of sweets."

Marina heard the child giggle and then the sound of the kitchen door slamming, and Carlos, bending his head as he walked through the low doorway, came towards her.

"New mattresses," he said cheerfully. "Pail, scrubbing brushes and soap. What more could you ask?"

He was smiling as he spoke, but Marina's mouth was set in a hard line and her eyes faced him defiantly. This was the moment, she thought, when she was going to tell him exactly what she thought of this whole ridiculous performance—this pretence that they were married; the suggestion that she should mend the performers' clothes, most of all the apparent insistence she should scrub out this van.

Then before she could speak, with one quick stride Carlos was at her side and taking her into his arms. She heard his voice say:

"Darling, I have been waiting to do this for hours."

Before she could move, before anything she had wanted to say passed her lips, his mouth was on hers.

She felt the strength of his arms round her shoulders, the hunger and insistence of his kiss, and everything was forgotten. The world was golden, the sunshine so glorious that her eyes were blinded and so she must shut them.

She didn't remember that they were in France, she couldn't even recall the circus or the caravan. She only knew that an ecstacy beyond words, more wonderful and glorious than anything she had ever dreamed of, swept her away into a state of happiness so intense that her whole being hurt from it.

She could be conscious only of Carlos's arms, his lips and the nearness of him. His love swept her from the world into a heaven of their own. She felt his kisses growing fiercer and more intense and knew that if she opened her eyes she would see the fire in his.

He was holding her passionately, possessively. He was the conqueror because the woman he loved had surrendered herself utterly to him.

"I love you! Oh God, I love you!"

He was saying over and over again as he kissed her eyes, her cheeks, her ears, the little pulse that was beating at the base of her throat, and then again, her mouth.

"I love you. I want you. I thought that we would never be alone together."

How long they stood there, locked in each other's

arms Marina had no idea. She only knew that at length, being human, it was impossible to sustain the intensity of their feelings and she broke away from him, breathless, but with glowing patches of colour in her cheeks, her eyes shining at him.

"Oh, Carlos!" She hardly breathed the words through lips that were soft and yet a little bruised by the hunger of his lips. "I love you."

"Say it again," he asked.

"I love you," she answered.

"Say it again and again and again. I want to hear it. I don't think I've ever heard you say it before."

He laughed at her, a laugh of sheer happiness.

"You're lovely," he said. "I adore your ridiculous tiptilted nose, the way your hair curls like red flames round your forehead."

"Tell me more," Marina whispered.

He took her back into his arms:

"I've got work to do," he said.

"Must you?" She gave a little cry. "You're not going to leave me?"

"Only to feed the horses," he said. "The head man is Hungarian—rather a nice chap—he said to come back in half an hour. It must be nearly that now." He glanced at his watch. "I'd better go. I don't want to get the sack the first day."

"But, Carlos, we must talk; we must . . ."

"I'll be back as quickly as I can," he said, "and, by the way, ask one of the children to get anything you want from the village—don't go yourself—send one of them, they'll do anything for a few francs—get tooth brushes, soap, towels, and of course, some pajamas for me and a nightgown for you. I wouldn't want you to feel shocked."

He bent and kissed her before she could expostulate, at the same time he pulled some notes from his pocket and thrust them into her hand.

"I'll be back just as soon as I can," he said, "and then we'll clear up this mess. I love you, darling."

He was gone before she could say any more, leaving her standing there bemused, the French francs clutched in her hand, her eyes following him almost disbelievingly.

Through the window she saw him running in the direction of the big tent.

"Can I 'elp you, dearie?"

The voice interrupted her reverie and Marina started.

Leaning against the doorway from the kitchen was a small, dark-eyed woman, holding a baby in her arms. Another Romany, Marina was sure of that before she answered.

"You're English."

The woman nodded.

"That's right. We've been with the Circus for over three years, my 'ubby and I."

"What does he do?" Marina enquired.

"Monkeys," the woman answered. "Fair daft on 'em he is; been training 'em all 'is life: father before 'im. Can't say I care for 'em myself." She paused and added: "I hear your 'usband's with the 'orses. A much nicer job if you ask me."

"Yes, I suppose it is," Marina replied.

She realised as she spoke there were other faces crowding round the caravan. They were nearly all Romany gypsies and she thought that perhaps Alfred Johnson found them good travellers and more at home on the road than other English people might have been.

"I see you've brought some mattresses," the newcomer said.

"Yes," Marina answered, "and now I suppose I've got to clean the caravan."

Even as she said it she realised that it was exactly what she was prepared to do. She no longer felt rebellious; she no longer wished to make other suggestions to Carlos.

He had won without a battle, without her even firing a shot in her own defence. She loved him. She loved him so much, she knew now, that if he asked her to walk barefooted from here to the North Pole she would set off happily without argument.

Resolutely she took off her jacket and smiled at her visitors.

"Will you show me where I can get some water," she asked. "The first thing I've got to do is to scrub this van from floor to ceiling."

Afterwards, she could never remember how much she had done or how much assistance she had had from her new-found friends. They had helped her; but it was actually she who had scrubbed the floor and polished the windows.

It was she who dragged in the mattresses as soon as the bunks on which they were to lie were dry; she who had spread on them the blankets which apparently Carlos had not thought necessary, and which she had found could be obtained, new, from Ma Johnson. She had sent a child for them and had been pleased to find them fresh and fluffy in cellophane coverings.

She had been so intent on what she was doing that it wasn't until the majority of her assistants had disappeared that she realised the time. With a little start she thrust the curls back from her forehead where they had flopped as she was scrubbing, and asked:

"What can be keeping my husband?"

"It's the evening performance," one of the women answered. "It starts at seven o'clock. You won't see him till it's over."

"That she won't," another Gypsy woman chipped in. "We're short handed and Handrathi never lets anyone leave until the animals are fed, watered and shut up for the night."

"What about food?" one woman asked. "There's nothing in your larder, you know."

"I hadn't forgotten that," Marina said.

Another child, with the promise of a franc, had set off for the village and had come back half an hour later with eggs, milk, butter, a small piece of veal, a long French loaf.

There had been coffee, too, which Marina had remembered at the last moment, but which, when she opened the tin, hadn't smelt anything like the aromatic coffee she was used to having with her breakfast.

A frying pan, a saucepan and kettle had all been obtained from Ma Johnson, who had sent back a message in response to the last request, that if anything else was wanted, the newcomer could wait till the morning because she was fed up with opening up her stores and she had better things to do.

"Take no notice of 'er," one of the Gypsies had said to Marina when the message had been relayed with gusto. "Her bark's worse than her bite. 'Sides, she don't like us buying them outside, 'cos then she loses her commission. That caravan of hers is stacked from floor to ceiling and she don't half carry on if she thinks she's losing her rake off on something expensive."

"She got me a radio last month," one of the women said. "I found afterwards I could have got it a pound cheaper if I'd gone to a shop."

"Yes, but they wouldn't 'ave given you credit," one

128

of the others said. "You know as well as I do, you're paying for it on the never-never."

"All the same, I think her takes too much," a woman complained.

There was a general murmur of agreement. Marina, on the other hand, could not help feeling grateful to Mrs Johnson.

It was all very well to start housekeeping from scratch, and Carlos, like all men, never realised how easy it was to forget that one needed towels, dusters, dishcloths and a teapot.

Fortunately she had not had to pay Mrs Johnson, and realised that all these expenses would go against Carlos's wages. It might have been uncomfortable to have to produce a Traveller's Cheque, and even worse, to try and change English pound notes which, she felt would make the whole position seem suspicious.

It was nearly ten o'clock when Marina sat down exhausted on the bed and realised that her back was aching as it had never ached before. Her hands, too, were stinging from the harsh soap and her knees were almost raw.

She had had the sense to take off her nylon stockings before she started scrubbing and she could not help wondering what Sybil would have thought if she could see her now, sitting utterly exhausted, with bare legs, on a gypsy's bed, feeling as tired as if she had cleaned out the Augean Stables rather than one small caravan.

And yet she had a great feeling of satisfaction which somehow alleviated her aches and pains. She had done it. She, Marina Martyn, who never in her life had so much as dusted a table or washed a cup and saucer, had cleaned out the whole caravan.

The place smelt fresh. The windows sparkled and

the kitchen shone, even though she had a suspicion that a great deal of that had been done by the other women.

"I've done it: I've done it," Marina murmured, and then with a little effort forced herself to go to the oil stove and start to prepare a meal for Carlos.

She was thankful that when she had been at school she had at least done a short course on cookery. It seemed years since she had last boiled an egg. She did know how to make a good omelette and she remembered how to salt and pepper the meat before she began cooking it.

A gypsy had brought her oil for the stove and one of them had lent her a big milk churn full of water.

"We've got enough, dearie," she said.

Marina thanked her profusely, being far too wise to offer her any money.

She wondered if her Mayfair friends would have been so generous or so helpful in the same circumstances.

She remembered in the past someone telling her what hard work it was moving house and how she had wondered why they had made such heavy weather of it.

Now, somewhat shamefaced, she recalled that the person, a girl with whom she had been at school, had been poor. She had obviously done it herself. Perhaps with her husband she had scrubbed out the rooms, hung the curtains, made the beds and at the same time remembered that it was time for meals.

A meal! With a guilty feeling, Marina remembered that her only contribution had been a bunch of expensive flowers scnt sometime later and then only because Sybil had reminded her to do it.

She broke the eggs into a bowl and left them ready to make the omelette when Carlos arrived.

She found herself listening for him, trying to hear above the noise of the merry-go-rounds the sounds which would tell her that the evening's performance in the big tent was ended. She listened and waited until, when finally he came, she was quite unprepared for it.

She had been alone, tired, conscious of her aching back and painful knees, and suddenly the door opened and he was there.

She forgot everything, turned from the stove and went towards him, her arms instinctively going round his neck. She drew his face down to hers and for a moment he held her very close without words as his lips sought hers. Then she realised that, he too, was tired.

"Are you all right?" she asked.

"I'm all right," he replied. "But I'd forgotten a bale of straw could be so damned heavy."

There was a hint of laughter in his voice before he looked towards the stove.

"And now, if I may say so, I'm very hungry."

"It won't take long," Marina said.

He went past her into the main part of the van.

"Good Lord!" he exclaimed: "what a transformation! Did you do all this?"

"Most of it," she answered.

"Darling, you're a wonder!" he said. "I was expecting to have to help you. How did you manage it?"

"Oh, it wasn't very difficult," Marina answered.

She heard her reply almost with amusement.

Then she knew she was no longer Marina Martyn, but just a woman like every other member of her sex who wanted to make a home for her man, wanted to cosset him and look after him and feed him.

She watched Carlos throw himself down on the bed with its new mattress and bright red blankets.

She heard him give a little sigh as he stretched his back.

"Supper will be ready in a few minutes," she told him and went back to the stove with a feeling of satisfaction which sent a glow of happiness coursing through her.

He had come home. They were together: nothing else mattered. They were together!

7

Carlos pushed back his plate with the age-old gesture of a man who has enjoyed his meal and feels satisfied.

"That was excellent," he said. "I'd no idea you were a cook."

Marina smiled. It was on the tip of her tongue to say she had only cooked for a few months at school and had sworn then that she would never touch a saucepan or frying pan again. Instead, almost coquettishly she replied:

"Why should you insult me by thinking I'm not a competent housekeeper?"

"You don't look the part," he answered. "Besides, I've seen your hands."

Marina held them up a little ruefully.

"They're not very elegant at the moment," she said. "Three nails broken and they're still stinging from the soap the gypsy child bought me in the village. It must be made of nothing but carbolic acid."

"That's why the caravan smelt rather like a sanatorium," Carlos joked.

"Don't you dare say a word against it," Marina answered. "I feel more proud of having got it clean than of anything else I've ever done."

"Who's done your cleaning for you in the past?" Carlos asked inquisitively. "I believe you told me your parents were dead, so it can't have been your loving mother. Was it a relation, or could you afford to pay?"

"Since I have a very good job, I've been able to pay," Marina said defiantly.

She picked up the dishes and carried them into the tiny kitchen.

When she went back, it was to find Carlos stretched on the bunk bed, his hands behind his head.

"I'm tired," he said. "I'm ashamed to admit it, but I am. There's one thing you can be certain of—I shan't attempt to seduce you tonight."

Marina felt herself start at the words. She had been so intent on cleaning the caravan, making up the beds, cooking the dinner, remembering all the things that were necessary for keeping house, that she honestly had forgotten that here in this tiny van she and a man to whom she was not married were to stay the night.

Abruptly because she was embarrassed, she slipped back into its place the table which was attached to the wall, and said sharply:

"I imagined I was dealing with a gentleman."

Carlos gurgled with laughter.

"You sound like something in a Victorian melodrama," he said. "Love doesn't wait for wedding rings and for introductions."

"If you're going to talk like that, I shall be sorry I came with you," Marina retorted.

"Darling, you have no choice," Carlos answered in his deep voice, "and I'm only teasing you. I love you; you know that. I'd never do anything you don't want. But it's not going to be easy—not if we're going to be here for long."

Marina didn't answer, and after a moment he held out his hand.

"Did you hear me?" he asked. "I love you."

She tried to resist him, but he was irresistible. Almost without conscious volition she put her hand in

134

his and he drew her towards him down on the bed. Then his arms were round her and he was kissing her.

"You're lovely, you're adorable," he said. "I should still love you, even if you were utterly useless, which makes it better and more marvellous that you can make me a home even in this tiny space."

He had drawn her onto his chest and now she raised her head and looked at him.

"Do you realise what a very short time we have known each other?" she asked.

"And yet we have crammed more into the hours we have been together than most people manage in years," Carlos replied.

Marina gave a little sigh, half of satisfaction, half because she knew that if he kissed her again she would forget what she wanted to say.

"Carlos," she said, "this is the first time we've been properly alone together, now tell me what all this is about. I've got to know."

"Yes, of course, you have," he said.

He edged himself up on the bunk, pushing a pillow behind his back, and then when he was sitting upright he put out his arms and drew her close again.

"I want to kiss you once again," he said. "I'm frightened that when I tell you my story you'll want to leave me. Do you really love me, Marina—or am I just a holiday interlude, a bit of excitement with which to pass the time?"

She shut her eyes because the touch of his hands and the sound of his voice made her thrill until it was hard even to keep her voice steady as she answered him.

"I love you; I love you as I've never loved anyone else before with all my heart."

"You're sure of that?" he asked. "You know nothing about me, remember. I may be an adventurer, a criminal flying from justice, someone who might spend the next ten years, if he were caught, in prison."

"I've thought of all those things," Marina answered, opening her eyes and looking at him, "and I know that whatever you tell me about yourself, however bad it may be, I'll still love you."

Carlos gave a deep sigh.

"I wanted to be sure of that," he said.

"You don't have to doubt me," Marina answered. "I do love you, I do. It's not something one can help or something one can stop. It's just there beyond reason, beyond logic if you like. It's more certain than anything else in the world. I love you."

He pulled her closer to him, pressing her head against his shoulder, but he did not kiss her. Instead he said in a dreamy voice:

"I've somehow dreamt love would happen like this. I've loved lots of women—you wouldn't expect me to lie about that. I've wanted them passionately. I've even told myself it was the real thing, what I was searching for, but always I've been disappointed or rather, I've always known at the back of my mind that something wasn't quite right. It may have been money, power or position, or it may have been that apart from being sexually attracted they weren't the right type for me. I don't know what it was: I felt that somewhere, some day I would find someone like you."

"I've felt the same thing," Marina said, "that's why . . ."

She stopped suddenly. She had been about to say "that's why I ran away," but then some inner caution, something cynical or suspicious which, for all her love of Carlos never quite vanished, made her bite back the words even as they reached her lips.

Suppose, after all this, he did know who she was? Suppose he had been clever enough to rouse her interest, to make her concentrate on him as she had never had time or opportunity to concentrate on any young man before? Supposing, after all, he was just another playboy?

Immediately the thought flashed through her mind she knew it wasn't true. No man who was not someone exceptional could have awakened her love as Carlos had done. No man could have made her feel that nothing else mattered; that whatever she did, however degrading the task, was an honour because it was for him and because she loved him.

Now she could anticipate what he was going to tell her. He had done something wrong. He was being chased, not by the ordinary forces of law and order of one country, but perhaps by the international police of the world, and if they caught him he would pay the penalty not perhaps by years of imprisonment but possibly by death.

She felt a sudden feeling of terror sweep over her and putting her arms round his neck, she pressed her cheek against his, hiding her face so that he could not see the anguish on it.

"I don't care what you have done," she said fiercely. "It may be wrong, it may be wicked, but I'll never leave you. Perhaps I may be able to save you. We'll run away somewhere safe out of Europe. Somewhere where these people, whoever they may be, will never find you. If we're away long enough, perhaps they will stop looking for you and forget you ever existed."

She was striving to give herself and him some courage, yet she was conscious, as she spoke, of being terribly and horribly afraid not for herself but for Carlos.

"D'you mean that?" he asked in a quiet voice. "You would come away with me wherever I asked you to go? You'd give up your friends, your relations, your life in England, just to be alone with me?"

"I'll give up everything," Marina answered.

She threw back her head and looked him in the eyes.

"Oh, Carlos, I thought I knew what love was; now I see it's so much bigger than I thought. To go with you would not be making any sacrifice."

He drew her close again and his lips sought hers; just for a moment she resisted him, almost impatient that he should have interrupted their conversation to kiss her, and then she felt the insistency of his mouth.

She found herself kissing back wildly and passionately and that anything he had to say wasn't really of any consequence. This was what mattered; they were together; they were one.

The ecstacy of touching each other seemed to light the tiny caravan as if all the stars had fallen down into it.

"I love you! I love you!"

The words seemed to be murmured over and over again, first by one and then by the other, and still their lips sought each other's and their bodies throbbed in unison.

Quite suddenly Carlos thrust Marina away from him.

"Go away from me, " he said. "What was it you asked me to be—a gentleman? Well, I feel very unlike one at the moment."

"Oh darling," Marina murmured.

He set her on one side; then swinging his legs off the bunk, he reached up and turned out the oil lantern with which the van was illuminated.

"Undress," he said. "Get into bed and when I come

back I'll tell you the story you have waited so long to hear."

"Where are you going?" Marina cried, frightened that he should leave her.

"I'm going for a last look at the horses," he answered. "I promised Handrathi that I would do so and I can't let him down."

"But Carlos, don't go now," Mariana spoke from the darkness and instinctively her hands went out towards him.

"I've got to go," he answered, and his voice was harsh. "Surely, you are woman enough to understand that."

Before she could say more he went out of the caravan and slammed the door behind him.

She jumped to her feet and through the uncurtained window watched him walk away into the shadows.

Already the lights in the caravans were going out, one by one. The merry-go-round was silent and there was only an occasional roar from the lions or a neighing horse proclaiming that some of the animals were still awake.

Because he commanded her, Marina undressed and slipped on the nightgown which the gypsy child had bought for her in the village. It was a cheap type of rayon patterned with flowers, and it had cost the equivalent of a few shillings, but the child had liked its gaiety.

It was too long for Marina, but otherwise it fitted her and, having cleaned her teeth with the new toothbrush and washed her face, she slipped under the blankets, wondering, because she had never slept without sheets before, whether she would find them rough and irritating to her skin.

Until she lay down she had not known how tired

she was, or how much her back ached. Carlos had complained of an aching back: Marina thought her's must be breaking; and her knees hurt her almost unbearably and yet she did not complain, not even to herself.

It had been worth this small suffering so that she could gain his approval, see the admiration in his eyes when he had come back to the van. He had enjoyed his dinner, though Marina doubted if he would have expressed so much appreciation had he not been so ravenous.

She tried to think back to all the things she had learned at her Finishing School. There had been a "Cordon Bleu" chef to teach the pupils how to cook. But she had spent most of her time giggling with her friends and doing as little as possible when it came to cutting up meat or drawing a chicken.

That everything had tasted well tonight was merely because she had been extravagant with eggs and butter and, by a piece of good luck, the meat the gypsy child had bought her had been succulent and tender before it was put in the pan.

Marina began to plan a list of things she had to buy the following day. What was more, she must remember to return the salt and pepper she had borrowed from the caravan next door and she must ask Carlos what he liked to drink. Tonight he had been content with coffee. He doubtless preferred wine or beer like other men.

"The moment I get up I'll make a list," Marina promised herself. . . .

She woke with a start, with the guilty feeling she had been asleep when she should have been awake. The sun poured into the caravan. Marina looked across at the other bed and sat up hastily. There was no one there.

140

The blanket was thrown aside, the pillow dented, and now she remembered. She had been waiting for Carlos to come back from seeing to the horses and had fallen asleep. How unfortunate, when he had promised to tell her the story she had waited so long to hear. How could she have done anything so stupid? And now he had gone out.

She reached for her watch, which she had set beside her on the windowsill, and saw it was only 6:30; but already there were sounds of movement outside. Dogs were barking, children were shouting and as she looked out of the window she saw that many of the caravan doors were open, the women sitting on the steps.

As she looked, she saw a woman bring out a plate of something and hand it to a child who came running across the grass to receive it.

"Breakfast," Marina said aloud. "Carlos will be back and wanting his breakfast."

She washed and dressed in her same clothes which were the only ones she had. She saw that sometime during the day she would have to wash her blouse and wondered if it would be possible to buy anything else to wear while it was drying.

Carlos's shirt would also want washing, she thought, and wondered exactly how one would wash a man's shirt and how it was possible to get an iron hot on a small oil stove.

She looked at her store of food and decided there were enough eggs left for breakfast. If she scrambled them they would go further. She started to get them ready just as there was a thump outside the door and Carlos came in.

He seemed to bring the freshness of the spring air in with him. He bent to kiss her just like any husband returning from the office, Marina thought; and then, as if his lips were not satisfied with her cheek, they sought her mouth.

"Darling, I'm so ashamed," she told him. "I fell asleep waiting for you."

"I know you did," he answered. "You were dead to the world when I got back. I knew as I heard you snoring that you wouldn't want to be wakened."

"I wasn't snoring," Marina said indignantly. "I know I don't snore."

He laughed and said easily:

"I'm only teasing. You were quiet as a little mouse, but I don't believe if you had snored like a grampus I'd have heard you."

"How did you manage to wake?" Marina asked.

"It's an old trick," he answered. "I taught myself during my campaigning days. I tell my sub-conscious what time I want to wake and lo and behold! it's better than any alarm clock."

"You might have woken me," Marina said reproachfully.

"I very nearly did," he replied, "but you looked so sweet, innocent and incredibly young, I just hadn't the heart."

"Another time, please waken me," Marina said. "It's wrong for anyone to work on an empty stomach."

"Yes, nanny," he answered.

He had started to open the cupboards in the tiny kitchen.

"What're you looking for?" Marina demanded.

"The razor you said you had bought me. You'll have noticed I need it."

"I had, as a matter of fact," Marina answered touching his chin. "You'll find the razor in that drawer, but eat your eggs first, they're nearly ready."

She managed to toast a piece of the bread from the night before, put it on a plate and poured the scrambled eggs over; but as she did so she realised that she had forgotten to heat the plate. Another time she would remember, she thought. It's very easy to forget to do all the things that one expects automatically from trained staff.

"Eat your eggs," she said, setting them down on the table and hurrying to prepare the coffee remembering as she did so that she should have started earlier so everything could have been ready at the same time.

"I'm afraid there's no milk," she said.

"It doesn't matter; I like it black," Carlos answered, his mouth full and then added in a voice of consternation:

"But what about you? You've left no eggs for yourself."

"I honestly don't want any," Marina replied.

"Nonsense!"

"No! I've got some toast and butter," Marina told him: "very fattening, but I've a feeling we shant need to diet on this trip."

She poured out his coffee and a cup for herself and took it into the van and sat down beside him and watched him with satisfaction finish off his scrambled eggs.

"I'm afraid there's nothing else," she said as he finished. "I think I had better go shopping right away; there's a mass of things I want."

"No," he answered.

She raised her eyebrows and he added:

"No, Marina; you are not to move from the caravan. I would rather you didn't go outside at all, but if you have to speak to the women keep near the door so that if you see any strangers about you can go inside and lock yourself in."

"Oh, Carlos! Is this really necessary?" Marina enquired.

143

"I'm afraid so," he replied.

"You were going to tell me all about it last night," Marina prompted, "but unfortunately, I fell asleep."

"We both needed our sleep," Carlos said sensibly. He glanced at his wrist watch:

"I've got a few minutes now and so I'll talk, but I've got to be back by 7:30 to help exercise the horses."

"They keep you busy," Marina said rather sarcastically.

"That's something I shall really enjoy," Carlos answered. "I can't tell you how much I've missed the feel of a horse between my legs."

He spoke with such feeling that Marina felt a pang of jealousy. She had only him; everything of her's was lost and he could find enjoyment in which she could have no part.

As if in his strange clairvoyant way he knew what she was thinking, he put out his hand. He took her tiny, pointed chin between his finger and thumb and raised it towards his face.

"I love you, darling," he said. "It's got to be enough because I have nothing else to offer you."

Marina pulled herself away from him.

"Tell me, tell me quickly," she said. "You'll have to go and I'll be left wondering what it's all about. It seems incredible that we should have been together so long and that I should not know."

"Very well," he answered.

He reached for a packet of cigarettes he had thrown on one of the windowsills and said:

"My real name is Carlos Ayelo de Coza."

He paused and looked at Marina and she realised he expected her to recognise the name. She did not attempt to pretend.

144

"I am sorry," she said, "I don't think I have ever heard the name before."

Carlos shrugged his shoulders.

"One thinks one is important," he said with a little sigh. "Never mind. My country is Culuna."

Marina knitted her brow.

"That does ring a bell," she said. "Culuna? I know, it's somewhere in South America, a small state."

"That's right," Carlos said encouragingly.

"I've heard of it," Marina said, "I know I have. Wasn't there something happening there a short time ago?"

Vaguely she could see a small paragraph in the paper—not a headline—nothing sensational.

"That's right," Carlos said again. "It was a revolution. It meant a lot to us, but not to anyone else."

There was a bitterness in his tone now and instinctively Marina put out her hand towards him.

"Tell me," she said; "Tell me from the very beginning."

"Very well," Carlos said. "Culuna is my country. My father was the President. Culuna is only a small country as South American states go, situated between Uruguay and Brazil. Our people were free and happy—or we thought they were."

Again there was that note of bitterness in his voice which made Marina tighten her fingers over his.

"Yes," he went on, "we thought they were happy until one day there was a revolution. It started as just a small uprising, the kind of thing which is always happening in South America where people are apt to be explosive and start shooting at the least provocation. This had happened before and nobody paid very much attention. But this time they shot my father."

"Oh, I am sorry," Marina murmured almost involuntarily.

"I'm telling this very badly," Carlos said, "because it's so difficult to put into words."

He gave a sigh before he continued:

"My father was Culuna. He had ruled over it nearly forty years. They loved him and they trusted him. We had never had any serious trouble in our country before. If anything went wrong, they always said: 'The Old Man will settle it'; and the Old Man did."

"Why should they have killed him this time?" Marina asked.

"He didn't realise it at first," Carlos said, "but this time it was a very different uprising from anything that had happened before. This time it was Communist inspired."

"What did they hope to gain by it?" Marina asked.

"Everything," Carlos answered. "They hoped to sweep the country, make it a Communist state between Uruguay and Brazil—can't you see the advantageous position they would be in?"

"But could they do that?" Marina questioned.

"That's the whole point," Carlos said eagerly; "that was why I had to come away. I got out with a few seconds to spare—otherwise they would have killed me too. I didn't want to go. I argued and argued against it, but the only Statesman with any brains, Pedro Laydos, who you might say was the Foreign Secretary in my father's regime, insisted on taking me to safety."

"Thank Heaven he did," Marina murmured, thinking of Carlos being shot and dying from a Communist bullet. "By dying you could have helped no-one."

"Yes, I could see that," Carlos answered, "and yet

I felt I had to stay and rally the people. But Pedro said it was too soon and besides, we needed help."

"What sort of help?" Marina enquired.

"Pedro has gone to the United Nations," Carlos explained. "He is asking for troops. He has to convince them that this is not an internal war, but something far bigger, part of the Communist plan for South America."

"Do you think he can do it?" Marina asked.

"If anybody can do it, Pedro can. I wanted to go with him, but I should only be hampering him. He was quite frank in saying that he did not want me and I should only make things more difficult."

"Why? Surely, they would listen to you," Marina said.

Carlos shook his head.

"They are far more likely to listen to Pedro. They know him and he is very experienced at that sort of thing. Besides, the one thing I had to do was to stay alive. As you know, they quite obviously were looking for me at Estoril."

"They? Who do you mean by 'they'?"

This was the question which had been troubling her mind for what seemed so long.

"Their Communist agents over here," Carlos answered. "Can't you understand? In Culuna the revolutionaries are well aware that as long as I'm alive there will always be numbers of my father's supporters and the people themselves who will rally to a de Coza. Dead, there is every chance of a dictator succeeding simply because there is no other rallying point."

"Yes, I can see that now," Marina said; "but Carlos, aren't you taking terrible risks?"

"Of course I'm taking risks," he answered almost angrily, "but what else is there for me to do? Pedro's instructions were that I was not to get killed. We tried to think of somewhere where no one would expect to find me. We chose Estoril because the aeroplane in which we fled from Culuna came down at Lisbon. We hoped that no one knew I was on it. Someone must have given me away. That's why the Communists followed us into your hotel."

"They killed that couple who took our sleeper on the train," Marina said in a voice barely above a whisper.

"And they were aware that we were in Paris," Carlos continued grimly. "You see, Marina, I'm one against so many, and we don't know whom we're fighting. The woman in the next caravan may be one! Who knows where the Communists are or where they hide? France is riddled with them."

"You mean they have sent out an instruction over the whole country to find and kill you?" Marina asked.

"That's about it," he answered, "so we've got to be too clever for them."

He smiled at her, then brought his clenched fist down on his knee.

"I've got to go back to Culuna," he said. "Can't you understand, I've got to save my people from these swine. They trust me, they loved my father and many of them love me. That was the whole object in leaving, to help my people."

He got up from the bed and walked across the tiny van.

"There's so much to be done," he said. "My father was splendid, but he'd grown old and he found it easy to let things slide. There had been dissentient voices in our Parliament—and quite rightly too. There are not enough schools. We want training colleges and hospitals. We want a chance to start up industry so as to bring prosperity. All this can be done and I would have done it when the time came. But I couldn't make my father undertake a programme like that. He just wouldn't understand."

Marina said nothing, and after a moment Carlos added almost angrily:

"I'm not excusing him to you. In his own way he was magnificent. He kept the peace in Culuna ever since the war and the majority of the people were happy. It was only when the Communists started their insidious campaign telling the people of the benefits other countries were getting that they grew restless."

"You really believe you can win it back?" Marina asked, going directly to the point.

"If I don't believe that," he answered, "I should walk out of here and let the Communists kill me. I know exactly what we should have, exactly what start we should make on a proper foundation for progress. It's certainly not what they have at the moment, a police state with bloodshed and violence, with spying and counter-spying. My people would never stand for that."

He moved back to the bed and sat down beside her.

"They're kind, gentle people," he said softly as if he was explaining to a child. "They laugh because they're happy. They smile because they have enough food and the women are pretty. The greatest ambition of a man is to have a good horse and a small farm. There is a great deal we can do to encourage the beef farmers; there is a lot to be done in the towns as regards rebuilding."

He set his chin in a hard line.

"I can do it," he said, "I can give them everything they want, but first of all I've got to get rid of their conquerors. These evil men who have crept in and seized power by killing and thieving."

He spoke almost like a visionary and looking at his face Marina knew he was inspired.

"You can do it," she said almost involuntarily, "I know you can do it."

"I know it, too," he replied. "If only Pedro can get the help we need, then I can go back."

For a moment Marina felt a loneliness such as she had never known in her whole life before. He had forgotten her, she could see that and she knew without his having to tell her, he would go without her if his plans for the future did not include her.

Just for the moment when talking of his country he had forgotten that she even existed. If he loved her, she was only second to Culuna where his whole being was centred.

Then the moment passed and Carlos said in a very different voice:

"That's my story. I'm sorry in some ways that you should have become involved in it. If I hadn't met you it would have been far better for you."

"I was meant to meet you," Marina replied. "Can't you understand, it was meant? If you hadn't been with me, those men might have found you alone and killed you. If you hadn't been thinking of me, you might not have been so clever in escaping from them."

"No, that's true," Carlos agreed. "You've been my guardian angel and what's more you've made me very happy."

He said it almost too easily Marina thought; then she felt his arm round her shoulder and he said:

"You've helped me more than I can ever explain. Thank you, darling, just for being you and for trusting me. It must have been hard not knowing what was at stake."

"And now?" Marina said, struggling not to be hypnotised by the deep caressing note in his voice, "What do we do now?"

"As soon as I get the opportunity I'm going to telephone Pedro, perhaps tonight, perhaps tomorrow. It's no use doing it too soon or he's not likely to have anything to tell me. These things take time, as everyone knows."

"If he has good news for you," Marina asked in a very low voice, "will you go back right away?"

"That depends," Carlos answered, "if the United Nations will send troops it's going to take time. If they give the usurpers an ultimatum—that may be another method of approach; but then I must be ready to appear to lead the loyal sections of my people against the Communists."

"You mean you will fight them?" Marina asked.

"Of course," he answered. "The army has been scattered. Some people in the towns have given in to what they think is the inevitable, but many loyal supporters have dispersed to the farms and to the outlying parts of the country where it will be very hard to find them. They will support me."

"But Carlos, think of the risk. What hope have you got . . . ?" Marina began and then the words died away in her throat.

Carlos had a look of dedication on his face as he said simply:

"We are going to win eventually, I know that in my bones. I have never been wrong when I have felt an absolute and certain conviction as I feel now. We shall win; we shall save Culuna. That's all that matters. My country will be saved."

Looking at him as he gazed with unseeing eyes across the caravan, Marina felt as though an icy hand took possession of her heart.

For she felt in the future which Carlos saw so clearly, there was no place for her.

8

As if a shutter suddenly came down, Carlos's expression changed.

"I've got to get back to work," he said, almost sharply. "Get me a pair of jeans; Handrathi says Ma Johnson has them. I think I'm a 32-inch waist and here's some money to pay for all the other things you want."

He pulled a great sheaf of notes out of his trouser pocket and Marina gave a little exclamation.

"Wherever did you get all that from?" she asked.

"I changed some of my Portuguese money with Maman at the Rue de Dupont," he answered, "and Handrathi has changed the rest. He won't talk; I told a long yarn about having a temporary job in Portugal."

"Shall I say we have come from there if any of the Circus people ask me?" Marina asked.

"Say as little as possible," Carlos advised. "As a matter of fact, those who travel with a circus don't ask questions for the simple reason that they themselves don't like being asked them."

His last words were almost shouted as he passed through the kitchen and then the caravan door slammed behind him and Marina saw him running across the grass outside.

She stood watching him until he was out of sight; then she sat down on his unmade bed and tried to sort out in her own mind what he had told her.

"So that was the explanation."

She had never imagined anything so frightening, and yet at the same time there was a satisfaction in knowing that he was not a petty criminal. She had not really believed that he could be, and yet somehow, the nagging doubt had been there.

"I'd have loved him whatever he had done," she whispered to herself, but she knew it was a relief to realise that there was nothing personal about this.

Now, at last, so many things were understandable. His air of authority; the way she had known from the very beginning that he was used to command; the manner in which he had passed through every crisis without panic. It was all part of his personality and he had recognised this subconsciously.

All the same, she was human enough to be glad that her estimation of him was right; and then, like an icy hand clutching at her heart she knew without being told that, as far as he was concerned, she had no place in his future.

She had known it in the way he had spoken of his country and of his desire to return immediately once he got help from the United Nations. She had seen it in the expression on his face and that visionary look in his eyes.

He loved her: she dared not think otherwise and yet his love was a very secondary thing to his adoration for his country or to his conviction that only he could save his own people.

Just for a moment Marina looked bleakly ahead of her, staring at nothing, into a loneliness that seemed a dark pit, the kind of hell she had believed in as a child. Then she threw herself down on the bed, burying her face in the pillow that Carlos had slept on last night.

She could smell the expensive hair lotion which he

had used in Estoril until they had been forced to run away without any luggage. The fragrance of it brought the tears to her eyes because it was so essentially him and she loved him so desperately.

"I love you, Carlos, I love you," she whispered into the pillow: "please love me a little."

Even as she said the words she heard the voices of men pleading in the same manner with her. She could hear Victor, the expression on his face one of incredulity, when she had told him she could not marry him.

"I'll make you love me," he had said. "What you expect is too much. Love isn't like that, except in the story books."

She had known then that he was wrong and that love could be an overwhelming, all-consuming fire; she had known instinctively that it would be a tempest that would sweep her off her feet, but always she had imagined that the man she loved would love her in return.

She had always been the one who was loved; always the one who had said No; always the one who had kept apart from the ardour, the passion and the pleading of those who sought to marry her.

Now the position was reversed. She was the one who loved, and though Carlos loved her a little, it was not enough.

She felt her love for him throbbing in every breath she drew, in the beat of her heart, in the sounds that reached her ears from outside, in the very abandonment of her body as she lay on his narrow bed. With an effort Marina sat up.

"I'll make him love me," she told herself, and tried not to remember Victor saying much the same.

She picked up the money Carlos had left her, and put it in her handbag, thinking, as she did so, that the bag looked too expensive. Then slipping it over her arm she walked out of the caravan towards the part of the field where Alfred Johnson's red and white van stood flamboyantly important amongst its lesser and not so ostentatious companions.

The woman who had helped her with the scrubbing was standing at her caravan door holding her baby in her arms.

"Going shopping, luv?" she asked with a glance at the handbag.

Marina nodded.

"I've got to get something to wear while I wash this blouse," she said. "I'm ashamed to be seen in it."

She spoke in a friendly, easy tone. She had never had any difficulty in talking to people. She had on one occasion helped a cousin of hers fight a parliamentary seat in the north country. The majority of his constituents had been factory workers and miners, and the fact that he had won the seat had, he said, almost certainly been due to Marina's persuasive powers with the women.

"What a lovely baby," she said now, looking at the fat, dark-eyed child which the woman was cradling in her arms.

"He's my seventh," the woman answered.

"They say that's lucky, don't they?"

"It seems as if it's the truth. His father got a job with this set-up, the very day he was born."

"What does your husband do in the Circus?" Marina asked.

"Oh, he's cat tamer," the woman answered and, seeing Marina's look of surprise explained: "Tigers, you know, and panthers, if they have one. They're always called Cats."

"I didn't know," Marina told her. "Isn't it very dangerous?"

The woman shrugged her shoulders.

"It's what he's been brought up to, but he had a bit of bad luck. The circus where he worked for years broke up and his best animals died and he couldn't get work for months."

"Now the baby's brought you luck," Marina said with a smile.

"He 'as, bless 'is 'eart," the woman answered.

She gave the baby a tight squeeze which woke him up and he started to yell.

"Time for 'is bottle," she shouted above the din: "see you later."

Marina continued on her way towards Johnson's caravan. Some of the Circus folk she passed only gave her hard, curious stares: the majority smiled and answered her cheerily when she bade them good morning.

Mother Johnson's caravan was just beyond the Guvnor's, Marina had learned that yesterday. It was painted blue and white in contrast to her husband's and was higher in that a kind of super-structure had been built on top of it apparently to hold more of the goods Mrs Johnson kept in her travelling shop.

Marina knocked somewhat nervously. Mrs Johnson opened the door. She was a small, big bosomed woman who was getting on in years; but her hair was dyed a fiery red and her face was elaborately made up despite the fact she wore only an old pair of slacks with a shapeless white pullover.

"Bit early aren't you?" she said disagreeably.

When she saw who it was her manner changed.

"Oh, your husband's with the horses, isn't he?" she smiled. "He bought the mattresses off me yesterday. Well, I hope you've got some money because I'm not giving you any more credit, not until the week's out, at any rate."

"I have the money," Marina said, a little stiffly.

She wasn't used to being told her credit wasn't good and it took her a moment to realise that Mrs Johnson was being sensible, not just unpleasant.

"Come in then."

Marina followed Mrs Johnson into the caravan to stand amazed at the manner in which it was packed from floor to ceiling with bales of material, boxes, plastic bags, pans and every sort of container which would ensure that the goods they covered would be carefully stored away without being damaged by the movement of the van.

"Good gracious! what a lot of things you've got here!" Marina exclaimed.

Mrs Johnson looked around with satisfaction.

"Got pretty nearly everything," she said: "there aint much that people ask for that I can't supply."

"What a good idea," Marina enthused. "It saves the people you employ having to shop in strange towns and perhaps being cheated."

"That's exactly what I said to Mr Johnson," Mrs Johnson replied. "I says to 'im, 'What's the point of them taking time off to go wandering round foreign towns?' and he knows as well as I do that they spend every penny they make, so they might as well spend it with us as give it away to strangers."

"Don't they ever save?" Marina asked curiously.

"Save? Don't make me laugh!" Mrs Johnson emitted a peculiar sound which might have been described as derisive amusement. "When they get paid at the end of the week, if they can't buy something they gamble."

Marina thought of the woman she had just spoken to with her seventh child. She was obviously the type who didn't take a thought for the morrow.

"That's why it's best for them to be in debt," Mrs

158

Johnson confided and added: "though why I'm telling you this I can't think. I suppose it's because you don't look like one of them. Where d'you come from?"

"My husband and I have only just got married," Marina said a little hesistantly. "I have never worked in a circus before."

"Well, apparently your man knows quite a lot about horses," Mrs Johnson said. "Handrathi was telling Mr Johnson this morning that he had been quite a help."

"I am glad to hear that," Marina said. "Yes, he knows a lot about horses."

"Well, I must say, it's nice to see someone from England," Mrs Johnson said. "We've brought some of our old people with us, of course, on this trip, though a lot of them don't like the foreign parts, it makes them nervous. Those we have picked up over here are the real travelling sort—Poles, Czechs, Italians. As I said to Mr Johnson, 'The Circus is nothing but a tower of Babel.'"

Mrs Johnson was looking Marina over as she spoke.

"You look smart," she said unexpectedly, "though I see that skirt's had a bit of rough usage. I expect you want to buy an iron, don't you?"

"That's one of the things I do want," Marina answered.

"D'you come from London?" Mrs Johnson enquired a little too casually for it not to be a leading question.

"I have worked in London," Marina answered.

"What at?" She saw the expression on Marina's face and added quickly: "Oh, I'm not prying, don't you think that; but I'm not going to say I'm not curious. We don't often get people as look like you hanging on to a Circus."

"Oh, I'm very ordinary," Marina told her. "My husband is South American."

She said it proudly, thinking to distract attention from herself, and realised as she said it that it might have been extremely indiscreet. Suppose anyone was making enquiries. She cursed herself for her stupidity, but there was nothing she could do. The words were spoken and she knew Mrs Johnson was listening with interest.

"Is he indeed?" was the answer. "I never got to South America, myself. But I've often thought it'd be a bit of fun to go there."

"D'you mean with the Circus?" Marina asked, hoping to change the object of interest from Carlos to herself.

"Oh, I wasn't always in the Circus," Mrs Johnson replied. "As a matter of fact I was in a trapeze act. I 'ad two lovely chaps with me. 'The Domino Trio' we called ourselves. We used to play the Music Halls and then they thought there was money in the circus. We travelled with two or three different ones—went to Germany, Spain, the north of Italy, France of course. We even got as far as Poland in one show—that was before the war."

"Did you enjoy it?" Marina asked.

She was trying to visualise Mrs Johnson swinging from a trapeze and finding it difficult.

"It paid when you were in work," Mrs Johnson answered simply. "And then one night the boys had a bit too much to drink and they dropped me. It broke my leg and I lost my nerve, and I was never much good after that."

"How awful," Marina commiserated.

"Well, it wasn't really," Mrs Johnson smiled, "You see I was getting a bit too old, only I didn't like to admit it, and Alfred—that's Mr Johnson—had been hanging about some time, so I married him and I must say I've never regretted it."

"What a wonderful story!" Marina exclaimed. "You ought to write a book."

She said the last words almost automatically; it was the kind of thing one always said at a party to a person who related an exciting adventure or told the story of their life.

"Well, I don't know about that," Mrs Johnson replied obviously taking the idea seriously. "I'm not all that good at writing; I've never got down to real lessons as you might say. Not that it's ever worried me."

"No, of course not," Marina said quickly.

"I'll tell you one thing though," Mrs Johnson continued, "I can add. People don't manage to squeeze much out of me if it comes to buying and selling."

She spoke aggressively as though people had often tried.

"And what was it you wanted?" Mrs Johnson enquired sharply. "That's a pretty handbag you've got there."

Her eyes were trying to size it up and Marina was certain she was guessing at the price.

"My boss gave it to me as a wedding present," she said quickly.

"My husband said you were a bit hard up yesterday, had to pawn your wedding ring," Mrs Johnson said. "I'll buy that bag off you if you want to part with it."

"Oh, I don't think my husband explained properly," Marina interrupted. "We had to pawn the wedding ring because we had had some money in another currency and we couldn't get it changed."

It sounded a bit lame even to her own ears, and

she thought almost angrily how tiresome it was of Carlos to involve her in so many lies.

"It's all right now?" Mrs Johnson asked.

"Yes, as a matter of fact it is. I've got French francs to pay for anything I buy."

"That's all right then," Mrs Johnson said almost in a disappointed tone, "but if you want to part with that bag, don't forget to let me know."

"I won't," Marina answered.

She began to choose the things she wanted. She found a blouse for herself and a cardigan she could slip over her shoulders if it got cold in the evenings. There was also a skirt she couldn't resist because it was so bright and colourful—a kind of gypsy skirt with flowers in bright colours appliqué'd on a black ground.

She bought the jeans that Carlos had wanted and a red and white check shirt which she felt would make him look exactly like a cowboy.

And then there were things for the caravan—sheets, coarse unbleached cotton ones, towels, glass cloths, saucepans, dishes and innumerable other small things which up to now she had always taken for granted, they used to appear like magic in her life. She had no idea how important they were until they did not exist.

She even found a pair of sandals, low and comfortable which she could walk about in instead of her high-heeled lizard shoes, and a pair of comfortable leather slippers for Carlos which because she was not certain of his size Mrs Johnson said she would change if they didn't fit.

By the time Marina had finished ordering a great pile of things stood on the floor.

Mrs Johnson, with unexpected generosity, offered

to lend her some curtains for the windows until she had time to make some new ones.

"They've been washed," she said, "they're clean. You don't want everyone peeking and prying in. I know when one's first married one wants a bit of privacy."

She gave Marina a dig in the ribs with her elbow as she spoke and laughed in a knowing way.

"Don't blush, dearie," she said. "I'm not so old that I can't remember what it's like to be young and he's a nice looking lad that man of yours."

"We're very grateful to your husband for giving him the chance of working here," Marina said feeling that the statement was somehow expected of her.

"Mr Johnson wouldn't employ anyone if he didn't think they'd pull their weight," Mrs Johnson answered and added: "though I must say, it was a bit of luck for you we were short-handed. It isn't often the Old Man lets anyone touch his precious horses, not unless he knows all about them."

"Thank you for all your help," Mariana said.

She drew the francs from her bag and realised as she did so that Mrs Johnson was having another look at the bag with an almost envious expression in her eyes.

"If I had another one I'd give it to her," Marina thought to herself and made up her mind that if she and Carlos ever got out of this mess she would send Ma Johnson the most beautiful bag she could find in the whole of London.

"Now, you can't carry all this," Ma Johnson said, looking at the pile of things they had accumulated on the floor. "You go back to your caravan, and as soon as Jim—that's my stepson—appears, I'll send him round with it. He won't be long; they're having trouble with the organ on the merry-go-round; as soon as he's got it fixed he'll bring them along to you."

"That's very kind," Marina said, "but I'll just take the blouse and skirt with me, it'll give me the chance to get the one I'm wearing washed."

"You have got it in a bit of a mess," Ma Johnson agreed. "What've you been doing? Kissing the coalman or something?" She laughed at her own joke and Marina wondered what she'd say if she told her she and Carlos had been climbing over the roofs of Paris, to escape from two men who were trying to murder them.

Marina picked up the things she wanted and as she did so another woman, dragging a small child by the hand, came into the caravan. She was Italian and started to ask in very broken English if Mrs Johnson had shoes for the child.

Marina slipped away, throwing the blouse and skirt she had chosen over her handbag as she was suddenly embarrassed by its obvious opulence and luxury.

She began to plan how it would be best for her not to take her handbag with her another time, but put her money in the pocket of her skirt if there was one, or even carry it in some way in her hand.

Because Ma Johnson had made her feel she looked different from the other circus people, she edged close to Mr Johnson's caravan, passing behind rather than in front of it. As she did so she heard his voice through an open window aggressively:

"What right have you got to come asking me questions about my employees?"

She stopped suddenly. Could this question concern Carlos? She had the feeling that it did. Then a voice, in good English spoken with a strong foreign accent, said:

164

"I was only asking if you had taken on anyone new to work for you yesterday or today?"

"I've already asked you who the devil you are," Alfred Johnson bellowed.

"I have my instructions, sir, to make enquiries."

"You're the police?"

There was an obvious pause before the man said: "Not exactly."

"Then get to hell out of it. I'm not answerable to anyone in this country except the police. I have my permits; my papers are in order and so are those belonging to the families I employ."

"But, sir, all we ask is a little co-operation."

"Which you're bloody well not going to get," Alfred Johnson answered. "I know your sort, snooping around frightening the men who are doing a good job. What are you, the Gestapo? Well, I haven't any room for you on my Circus. Get out and be quick about it."

"You'll be sorry for this. If you're helping the man we seek," the foreign voice said. "He'll be either alone or with a girl. She's of no importance, but he's wanted."

"By whom?" Mr. Johnson enquired. "Let me see your papers, show me your warrant, if you've got one."

There was a moment's silence and it was obvious that the men to whom he was speaking could produce no papers. Then Marina heard the scrape of a chair as if Alfred Johnson rose to his feet:

"Get out of here!" he said, "and don't let me find you trying to get information out of my men. If you do, I'll break your necks, both of you. I'm within my rights and you know it. March!"

He must have been towering over them, perhaps moving towards them in a threatening manner.

Marina heard the clatter of footsteps as they crossed the caravan and stepped out on to the grass. She realised her own position and running faster than she had ever run before she moved along the backs of the caravans, dodging round wash tubs, milk churns, perambulators and great piles of debris of every sort and description until she reached her own caravan.

Without looking to right or left she moved from the back of her van and through the front door in what was almost one quick movement. She closed the door behind her and stood for a moment leaning against it, her breath coming agitatedly through her lips both from fear and from the speed at which she had run.

So "they" had caught up with them. Nowhere was there any sanctuary. For a moment, in a blind panic, she thought she must run and find Carlos; then she realised that this was the most stupid thing she could possibly do. She must keep her head. She must wait until he returned, then they could go away. Where to? She had no idea. Once again they must be on the run.

For a long time she could do nothing but stand frightened and panting until there was a knock on the door. She jumped, and the blood drained away from her face leaving her deathly pale. The knock came again, and then before she could answer a voice said:

"Are you there? I've brought your stuff from Ma Johnson!"

Marina threw open the door with a little sigh of relief; it was only Jim Johnson, his arms filled with her purchases.

"Where shall I put them?" he asked.

"Oh, on one of the beds," Marina said, "thank you so much for bringing them."

"Got another load," he answered cheerily, "couldn't manage them all at once."

"Thank you so much," Marina answered, thinking with a pang as she spoke that she and Carlos were not going to need all these things. They would all be left behind and she was certain Ma Johnson would snaffle them all back and sell them to somebody else.

"Well, I'll get them then," Jin said. "This isn't a bad little caravan as it happens."

He looked round with an appraising eye.

"Yes, it might be worse," Marina said casually. "When we're rich, we'll buy one with electric light."

As she spoke she realised that Jim was staring at her with a look in his eyes she knew only too well.

"Come to that," he said, "at the next stop I'll try and fit you up with a lead off ours. I'm the electrician round her and it shouldn't be too difficult."

"That's very kind of you," Marina answered. "I'll tell my husband, I know he'll be most grateful."

"That remains to be seen," Jin said, with a twist to his lips.

Marina guessed as he turned away that many of the husbands were not too pleased when Jim provided special favours for their wives. He was the type of young man, cocky and sure of himself and with an abundance of virility which one could find in every walk of life and who was, inevitably, attractive to the opposite sex.

When Jim came back with the second load he stood for a moment, his hands on his hips, his head almost touching the ceiling of the van.

"Do I get any payment for my labours?" he enquired.

"Of course, if you want it," Marina replied. "I thought, being the son of the boss, you were too grand to tip."

"I wasn't talking about money," Jim answered.

He tried to catch hold of her, but she was too quick for him.

"I'm expecting my husband home at any moment," she said warningly. "I warn you, he's very jealous."

"Well, let's give him something to be jealous about," Jim answered coming towards her to where she had retreated in the small kitchen.

"You flatter yourself," Marina said.

She opened the door of the caravan as she spoke and stepped outside. Jim couldn't very well assault her in the open and, still grinning, he followed her out.

"First round to the lady," he said mockingly, but in a lower tone, so that the women standing in the adjacent caravans could not hear him.

"I'm not entering for another round," Marina retorted.

She stepped back into the caravan and shut the door.

She would have trouble with Master Johnson, she thought grimly if they were going to stay long, but obviously that complication was not going to arise.

She put away the things on the bed perfunctorily, not really interested. As soon as Carlos came back, they would be gone and then she remembered that whatever happened they would need to eat.

"What a hopeless housekeeper I am!" she chided herself, thinking how pleasant it would be just to ring the bell and expect a well-cooked three-course meal to appear automatically.

She went out and looked for the gypsy girl who had done the shopping for her the night before. The child fortunately only lived two caravans away and was engaged in looking after four small children whose ages seemed to range between six months and six years. When Marina asked for help, she was only too willing to take instructions.

The five francs she had received the night before for her pains was a *pourboire* out of all proportion to anything she had received in her life before.

She left the six-year-old in charge and came back to Marina's caravan.

"Quite sure your mother won't mind you doing this for me?" Marina asked anxiously.

"Naow, she won't mind," the child answered, "she's gone to the village to get a drink. That's all she cares about."

It was a simple statement of fact. Marina felt her heart contract. There was nothing she could say or do which would make things better.

"Shall I write down the things I want?" she asked.

"Naow, I can't read," the child answered. "Just tell me slowly; I'll remember them."

Marina said her requirements over twice and handed the child the money, and with a little frown between her eyes, watched her hurry off.

"Why didn't I know about people like this before?" she asked herself. "I could have helped them."

She wasn't quite sure how because obviously money wasn't the solution. To those who spend every penny they earn and those who drank, money wasn't any help. But it seemed wrong that a child of twelve should not be able to read or write.

It was all very well for Ma Johnson, who was of a different generation, to have had no schooling, but now, with the schools that were springing up like mushrooms all over England, surely these gypsy children ought to be educated too.

An hour later she was still turning the problem over in her mind when the girl returned. She had forgotten nothing and Marina rewarded her as she had done the night before with a five franc piece. The child snatched at it and then hesitated:

" 'Ere," she said, "you're one of us, so I should tell you you don't have to give me so much. A franc would be plenty, that's about one and threepence, you know."

Marina stared in surprise, then she said, almost fiercely:

"I want to give it to you; you have helped me, and perhaps it'll help you. Don't let your mother have it. Keep it in case you and your brothers and sisters ever want anything."

"I'll do that," the child said, "and thank you, you're nice. I wish I looked like you."

It was the cry of every woman who has ever seen one of her sex looking pretty and glamorous and making her in contrast feel unattractive.

Marina looked down at the small wistful face with its swarthy skin, dark eyes and tangle of black, unbrushed hair.

"You can't look like me," she said, "because I am fair; but one day, when you're a little older, you'll be very attractive. I'm not a gypsy, but I can tell your fortune; because you are kind and helpful and because you are a very sweet person everybody you meet will love you. Will that make you happy?"

In response the child suddenly threw her arms around her.

"You're so pretty," she whispered and then, like a wild animal, she turned and ran from the caravan.

"How can I have children like that?" Marina found herself asking the question over and over again as she prepared a meal for Carlos, making a fragrant stew with the meat, mushrooms and onions which the child had bought her in the town.

It was just ready when she heard him open the

door, and before she could speak or greet him he caught her in his arms and was kissing her hungrily and passionately as if he hadn't seen her for a long time.

"I love you," he said when his lips left hers. "Did I forget to tell you that this morning? It's very important. Shall I say it again? I love you."

As always when he touched her she felt the magical thrill that he could evoke ripple over her until it was hard to think coherently, and yet at the back of her mind she remembered all too clearly that she was a very small and transitory part of his life.

"I have something to tell you," she said. "Something very frightening."

"What is it?" He released her immediately and his voice was sharp.

"They've been here," she answered. "Two men. I heard them speaking to Mr Johnson."

"Are you sure? What did they say?"

She told him what she had heard through the open window of Alfred Johnson's caravan. She told him how the two men had been routed and sent away without any information.

"Good for Johnson!" Carlos exclaimed.

"Don't you understand?—they won't stop there," Marina said. "He told them not to snoop about the place, but of course they will, and someone is certain to tell them we only arrived last night. We must go at once."

Carlos moved from her side and sat down at the table.

"Let me think," he said.

"You've got to eat, anyway," Marina said.

She helped him to stew and saw with satisfaction that the meat was well done and tender and that it smelt delicious.

"I may be wrong," Carlos said after a moment, "but I'm almost certain they'll get nowhere if they question the circus people. As I told you this morning, they keep their mouths shut."

"Suppose they bribe them?" Marina asked.

"I doubt if they'd accept bribes," Carlos answered. "There is a sort of code against giving up the man who is wanted to the authorities, and they're certain to think these men are police."

"It was clever of Mr Johnson to ask to see their warrant or their credentials," Marina said.

"Johnson must have been up against this sort of thing hundreds of times," Carlos answered, "and he certainly won't want to lose any of his staff. At the same time, this is the red light. We can't stay with this lot too long; but I think we are safer here than most places. We're moving tonight, by the way."

"Moving?" Marina questioned.

"Yes, our next stop is Dijon, about 80 kilometres away. We move as soon as the evening performance is over. It means, of course, we're on the go all night. I thought I knew about hard work until I joined this lot. I'm learning."

Carlos spoke with a smile and Marina saw his plate was empty.

"It certainly makes you hungry," she said.

"Sit down and have something to eat yourself," he commanded. "Things always seem worse on an empty stomach, we all know that."

She obeyed him, not because she felt hungry but because it was so pleasant to be sitting opposite him in the caravan eating stew and cutting slices off the long, crisp French loaf.

"Is there anything else?" Carlos asked pushing back his plate.

"Cheese," Marina answered.

She rose and fetched a Camembert from the kitchen and turned it onto a plate.

"No one could make a better travelling companion," Carlos said, "you think of everything."

"I'm afraid I forgot you might want something to drink," Marina answered; "you'll have to be content with coffee."

"I'll choose my own wines when I get the chance," he answered.

He watched her pour the coffee into the cup, then said quietly:

"Are you frightened—by what happened this morning?"

"I am rather."

"I ought not to have got you into this," he said.

"I don't regret it," Marina said quickly. "Don't think for a moment I regret having met you or anything that has happened. It's only I am so frightened they may kill you. Oh, Carlos, can't we go anywhere that's safe?"

"D'you suppose I hadn't thought of that?" he asked.

"This morning when I was exercising the horses, I thought of nothing else. Thank God, there was quite a mob of us. I'm certain that our safety lies in always being with people. That's why I don't want to abandon this refuge if I can help it."

"I am getting almost to love our little caravan," Marina said. She hesitated before the last word: she had almost said "home" but that seemed too obvious.

Carlos drank his coffee and lit a cigarette.

"Let's try and find a solution," he said. "I can spend the afternoon in proper continental style—in a siesta."

"You haven't any work to do?" Marina asked, her eyes lighting up.

173

"No, thank Heavens," Carlos answered. "I've done enough this morning to last me for a long time and tonight's going to be no picnic."

He put out his hands towards her as he spoke.

"Wait a minute," she said. "Ma Johnson lent me some curtains; let's put them up, shall we?"

"Ashamed of anyone seeing me kiss you?" Carlos asked.

"It's not only a question of being ashamed," Marina answered. "I would rather nobody saw us, especially the two men who are looking for us."

"Very well, then," Carlos answered in a resigned voice. "Where are these all important curtains? I'll put them up and then I'll kiss you. Is that a promise?"

"I'll think about it," Marina answered provocatively holding out the curtains to him.

He took them from her and as he did so he looked down into her eyes:

"Damn the blasted curtains!" he exclaimed, and threw them on the floor.

He picked her up in his arms and carried her to the bed where his mouth fastened on hers. Then he was kissing her wildly, passionately till Marina felt a flame awaken within her and she kissed him back, forgetting everything, the people who might look in, the danger that lurked outside and even the fact that she loved Carlos far more deeply than he loved her.

9

Carlos's lips felt as though they would draw her very soul from her body.

She felt his kisses possess her as if she had surrendered herself to him utterly and she was indeed a part of him. He seemed to squeeze the very breath from her. She felt as though she was drowning in a green sunlit sea, sinking deeper and deeper beneath the waters until she was utterly and completely submerged.

She felt his hands touching her body; and then piercing like a shaft of light into the darkness into which she had fallen, she knew that this was not the true way of love, but only the counterfeit she had met so often in her life before.

With an almost super-human effort she forced herself back to consciousness, compelled her brain to supersede the aching need of her body, and finally thrust Carlos aside, to rise to her feet.

"Don't move, darling," he said pleadingly: "I want you, I love you. There was never anyone like you in the whole world."

Words, words, Marina thought with sudden clarity; and yet he had not mentioned the one word she wanted to hear, the word which she knew would tell her his love was not a transitory thing but for ever.

She stood with her back to him fighting to control the throbbing in her veins, the weakness of her body which longed to throw herself beside him again and lift her mouth to his.

175

"Marina, come here."

The words were half command, half plea. Still she did not turn round. She knew that if she did she would be unable to resist him.

She could feel the magnetism of him reaching out to her; she could feel his will compelling her to obey him, and yet she knew she must resist it; not entirely in self-defence, because she would have given herself willingly enough; but because she knew, her hold on him being so precarious, she might in giving in to his desires lose the little she already had.

It was in that moment that Marina vowed with every force and feeling within her that Carlos should love her as she loved him. Never before had a man resisted her. Never before had she been the suppliant; but, she told herself, never before had there been a man so worth the winning, a man so well worth loving.

Forcing herself to speak lightly, she said:

"You go to my head, Carlos. I thought you had promised not to seduce me."

"You know I never promised anything of the sort," he answered. "I love you and I think you love me a little. Does anything else matter?"

"Quite a lot of things," she answered coldly. "Your country for one and my future for another."

"Darling, you know I wouldn't do anything to hurt you," Carlos said. "I promise you one thing, that if I come out of this alive, you'll never have to work again."

"Are you offering me money?" Marina asked softly. Carlos shook his head.

"No," he answered. "I am offering you security if possible, and that's a very different thing."

Marina turned round to face him.

"I thought you were clever," she said in a low voice. "I thought you understood women."

"Have I said anything wrong?" Carlos asked almost in the tone of a bewildered child.

"Not by your standards, perhaps," Marina answered, "but by mine, and that's very different. I have loved you because I couldn't help it. I wanted no reward for loving you any more than you expect me to reward you. It's something that has happened between us and there's no question of anything else."

"There's always the future," Carlos said with a little sigh.

"Your future may worry you," Marina said: "that's your problem. Please don't worry about mine."

"But of course I worry!" he exclaimed half angrily. "Do you seriously imagine that after all we have been to each other we could part without my thinking about you and worrying about you and making some provision for you if it's possible for me to do so."

Marina sat down on the bed opposite him, tucked a pillow behind her shoulders and swung her legs up onto the bed.

"You are thinking of something hypothetical," she told him. "Suppose we come down to brass tacks. What are we going to do? We don't just want to sit here and be killed—that'll provide for nothing except our graves."

"I want to forget all that for a moment," Carlos said. "And I can only forget it when I'm kissing you. Come back to me, Marina. Let me hold you in my arms. I promise I'll do nothing you don't want me to do."

"That's the problem," Marina said with a provocative smile.

Carlos sat up suddenly.

"Damn you!" he said. "You excite me, and then just when I think I have captured you and you belong to me, you slip away through my fingers. Who are

177

you? And what goes on inside that funny, lovely little head of yours?"

"Let's talk sense," Marina replied.

At the same time her heart leaped a little; at least he was intrigued by her. It was easy for a man's body to be excited by an attractive woman. It was far more difficult to excite a man's brain.

Carlos crossed the caravan to pick up a packet of cigarettes that he had thrown on the window sill.

"Why don't you change into the shirt and jeans I bought you?" Marina asked. "And then I think we'd be wise to put up the curtains."

"Damn it all, you sound like any suburban wife making her husband do his bit," Carlos grumbled; but he did as suggested, shutting the door into the kitchen as he changed.

He came back looking, as Marina had known he would, like a cowboy out of some very unrealistic film.

"The fit is perfect!" Marina exclaimed as he appeared. "You look so elegant, it's a pity you aren't part of the circus instead of just one of the grooms."

"Handrathi said the same thing," Carlos answered. "Perhaps I could go into the big tent: I can assure you I should be better than a great number of the performers. This is a pretty second-rate outfit."

"Nevertheless, they've been kind to us," Marina retorted, feeling on the defensive because the circus was English and Carlos was criticising it.

He had read her thoughts and laughed softly:

"All right, Miss Britain; I'll bow to the Union Jack and say the whole show is first-class, though God knows what Bertram Mills would say if I did."

"How do you know so much about our Circuses and everything else British?" Marina asked.

"I was taken to Bertram Mills' Circus when I was

178

at school," Carlos answered. "It seemed to me—though I suppose I saw it through bedazzled eyes—that it was the most fantastic and wonderful show on earth. I've never forgotten the horses. Poor Handrathi, for all his skill he can't produce anything like their performances."

"So if you never become President, you can be a bareback rider," Marina teased.

She saw at once that she should not have referred to Carlos's position even jokingly. His face darkened and he sat down on the edge of the bed drawing furiously at his cigarette.

"What are we to do?" he asked in a very different tone of voice. "I've got to try and get in touch with Pedro tomorrow. There's no use my telephoning him too soon. He'd have nothing to tell me. Tomorrow or the next day there might be news."

"In the meantime," Marina prompted, "you think it is dangerous to stay where we are."

Carlos said:

"I think that having no information about us at the Circus they will look elsewhere."

Before Marina could speak he suddenly jumped to his feet.

"Fool that I am!" he said; "I've got the solution. Why didn't I think of it sooner?"

"What is it?" Marina asked.

"Lisbon," Carlos answered. "Of course, we must go back to Lisbon. It's the last place they would expect to find us, knowing that we left there because they were on our track, and from my point of view, it's the one place I had better be when Pedro gets his answer."

"Why?" Marina asked.

"Because I can get an aeroplane from Lisbon to Buenos Aires and from Buenos Aires to Culuna. In

Paris or even in England there would be lots of changes all of which involve danger."

"Then surely they might think of that too," Marina suggested.

"Oh, it isn't obvious," Carlos said. "One can get aeroplanes to anywhere; but having run us out of Lisbon I have a feeling it is the last place where they will expect us to turn up."

"So I'm to come too," Marina said.

"Of course," he said sharply. "You don't suppose I'd leave you here, or even let you go back to England until I am out of their reach. You don't know what they're like. Besides, they would be certain to use the Nazi method of holding you as a hostage, or rather using you as a bait to lure me into their net. No, we stick together until both you and my enemies can see the very last of me."

Marina gave a little sob. It burst through her control and she couldn't help it.

"How can you talk like that and at the same time say you love me?"

Carlos sat down on the bed beside her and put his arms around her.

"Oh darling, darling," he said. "I never meant it to come to this. You looked so entrancingly pretty in the dimness of that cave and when I put my arms round you it seemed for a moment as though you had a right to be there close to me, against my heart; and then, when we went up into the sunlight, you were even lovelier than I had anticipated. I had been bored and miserable and terribly depressed until you came walking into my life."

He put his hand under her chin and turned her face up to him.

"I knew when we sat together at luncheon in that little café overlooking the Bay," he went on, "that you were very different from anyone I had ever met before. I could feel something happening to me, feel myself changing just because your eyes were looking into mine. Your hair was curling round your face like a fiery halo."

Carlos paused for a moment then bent his head to kiss Marina's lips gently and without passion.

"I don't think there could be another woman in the world like you," he said. "The way you behaved when we had to run for the train; the way you have never reproached me; the manner in which you have adapted yourself to this crazy adventure in a circus. Oh, Marina, you're a wonderful person and I haven't the words to tell you how marvellous I think you are."

Marina knew by the tone of his voice that he was suffering and though she longed to comfort him, she knew he must work out a solution for himself.

Because his lips were still near to hers and she longed for the touch of them, she said quickly:

"So we go to Lisbon; but how?"

Carlos took his arms from around her and reached for another cigarette.

"That's the question," he said simply. "And at the moment I'm not clever enough to find the solution."

"Will they be watching the airports?" Marina asked.

"I suppose so. They may imagine we'll try and get to England. You thought it would be safer there and they are very likely to think the same thing."

"What about trying to charter a plane?" Marina suggested.

She saw his eyes light up at the idea.

"You're a genius!" he exclaimed. "Why didn't I think of that before? But, of course, the trouble will be to find a small, unobtrusive aerodrome run by a company which carried passengers or freight. There must be dozens of them if only we knew where to look."

"Perhaps Handrathi will know," Marina suggested.

"He might," Carlos agreed. "He told me this morning this is the third year in succession they have taken this particular route with the Circus. He was complaining as it happened, saying that Alfred Johnson was getting old and afraid of breaking new ground in case it didn't pay as well as the old way."

"Well, ask him," Marina said. "I don't suppose there's any point in my talking to the women—they wouldn't know anything."

"We mustn't be too obvious about it," Carlos said. "I'm told that Johnson is furious if any of his men leave. He might turn spiteful and tell the gentlemen who called this morning what they wanted to know."

"If he does, I only hope we will be far away," Marina said. "What time do we move tonight?"

"Immediately after the last performance," Carlos answered. "In fact they start packing up as each turn comes off, getting the animal trucks hitched up to the tractors which pull them."

"What happens to us?" Marina asked.

"Handrathi tells me that is all arranged," Carlos replied. "The men who aren't actually concerned with the animals, attach the caravans to cars or trucks. A lot of the better turns have their own car, of course."

"I hope you don't go off with the horses and leave me behind," Marina said.

"I have to obey orders," Carlos said, and she wished that he had said it in a different way and had promised that he would never leave her.

"Tell me about your country," she suggested, asking the question, not only because she was curious, but because she wished for the moment at any rate to distract Carlos's attention from herself.

"It's very beautiful," Carlos said. "A perfect land for riding. In fact, one has to travel on horseback over the greater part of the land because there are no roads. That's another thing I have to see to. My father was old-fashioned. He hated motor-cars. He put every opposition he could in the way of men who wanted to open up the country. I would take the roads to the mines, to the river, into the mountains, where I believe there is gold and quite a lot of precious stones which we could sell to help finance new projects."

There was a light in his eyes and an enthusiasm in his voice which told Marina all too clearly how much this meant to him.

"The first thing is schools," Carlos went on. "We have got to educate our people; and there must be technical colleges so that we can make our own people do the developing of our country."

He suddenly brought his clenched fist down hard on the palm of his other hand.

"I'll drive every damned communist over the borders of my country or string them up from the trees. They only want to exploit the country: they wouldn't do anything for the people. I have seen the pattern too many times."

"How strong is this man who has taken your father's place?" Marina asked.

"He would never do that!" Carlos contradicted her fiercely. "He's only a weakling, a pawn whom the communists are using as a figure-head. My father may have been wrong and obstinate, but at least he was part of the country and he loved his people."

"Will they love you too?" Marina said.

"They will accept me if they get the chance, because I am my father's son," Carlos answered. "After that, it'll be up to me. I must teach them first to respect my regime and then to have an affection for me personally."

Carlos had that inspired, dedicated look about him again and Marina shut her eyes so that she should not see it. There was a long silence and she knew he had forgotten her completely. His thoughts were far away in his own country with the people he loved and whom he believed he must save.

With a jerky movement, because otherwise she felt she might cry out to him, Marina swung her legs to the floor.

"You have changed," she said lightly, "and I'm going to do the same. Just you wait until you see the gypsy skirt I bought myself this morning."

She changed as he had done, behind the door which led into the little kitchen. The mirror from her handbag was too small for her to see anything of herself except her face.

She knew by the look in Carlos's eyes how lovely she looked as she came back into the caravan wearing the pale pink blouse with its open neck and short sleeves, and beneath it the gypsy skirt with the vivid red roses and blue cornflowers scattered over its flared fulness.

Carlos held out his hand.

"You look enchanting," he said, "but alas! you don't look like a gypsy."

"I don't?" Marina queried.

"No," he answered. "You look like an angel pretending to be one. It's a very different thing. Come and kiss me. One ought to kiss someone one loves when they wear a new dress; it's an old Culuna custom."

"I don't believe a word of it!" Marina answered.

She let him kiss her, only compelling herself to draw away as his kisses grew more passionate. He tried to pull her down beside him on the bed.

"It's time for a cup of tea," she said hastily. "You must remember I'm English and even if you don't want a four o'clock cuppa, I do."

"We drink maté in Culuna like most of the South American countries," Carlos said. "I wonder if you would like it."

"It doesn't seem as if I'll get the chance to know one way or the other, does it?" Marina said.

"No," Carlos agreed, "my country will not be safe for tourists for a long time after this."

It wasn't the answer that Marina had expected and she felt her spirits drop as she went into the tiny kitchen to heat the kettle.

Once they had finished drinking the strong inexpensive tea the gypsy child had brought from the village, Carlos looked at his watch and said:

"I'd better go and see what's happening. I think Handrathi will want me. I'll be working with him from now until we start the move. If I don't come back don't worry."

"D'you mean I've got to stay alone in this caravan all night?" Marina asked.

"Darling, there isn't any alternative," he said.

"Can't I come and be near you?" she enquired.

She felt suddenly frightened. At least until now they had always been together.

"What can I do?" Carlos asked. "If I stay away, there'll be a row and Johnson might even chuck us out. That wouldn't help things at all. No, we must move with the crowd, and try and slip away if we can hear of some convenient aerodrome."

"I'll have our own clothes ready," Marina said.

"We couldn't very well travel like this. I'll press your suit and try and wash your shirt. I don't promise it'll be much of a success, though."

"You're marvellous!" he said, kissing her cheek.

"I don't feel marvellous," she answered with a little shiver. "I'm frightened. Oh, Carlos. I'm more frightened now than I have been all the time. It's because we're not together. It has been so different when you were there."

"I love you," Carlos said. "Don't you think it's agony for me to have to go away?"

"At least you've got something to do," Marina said almost to herself and didn't realize it was the cry of every woman since the beginning of time.

"I can only stay here in this stuffy little caravan and wonder what's happening outside," she moaned. "Suppose they shoot you and leave you, will anyone come and tell me?"

"You know they will," Carlos answered, "but no one is going to do that. Remember one thing, these men whoever they may be have never seen us. They are working blind, on instructions only."

"But will they have a photograph?" Marina enquired.

"It seems unlikely," Carlos answered. "There are photographs of me of course in Culuna, but I think there is a very remote chance that any of them have been flown over here. No, I can see quite clearly they were told that I might be in Lisbon. I had been there four days before they caught up with me.

I expect they tried every hotel, every boarding house to see if anyone had arrived who sounded like a South American. The two men who came to the hotel may have seen me, but I should think it unlikely.

One of them doubtless got on the train after we

had boarded it and learnt from the sleeping car attendant where we were supposed to be and struck blindly at the two people who were occupying our berths."

Marina gave a little shudder.

"I can't bear to think of the poor things," she said.

"At least they didn't suffer," Carlos said. "But to continue . . . After that, I think the trail must have been lost. The two men in Paris might have been the two who were in Lisbon, but, somehow, I don't think so. And the men you heard this morning might have been the two from Paris or two other agents working in a different area altogether. But you can be certain that knowing we had eluded them, the road south was not the only one they would cover."

"It's all so complicated, so frightening," Marina continued. "How many of them are there? Haven't they anything else to do but look for you?"

"Those are questions I'm not going to attempt to answer," Carlos said. "All I can promise you, as I said before, is that I have every intention of staying alive. Sooner or later people in Culuna will know they have been fooled. It takes time for news to travel because the country is backward; but when the people in the interior learn of my father's death, they will, I know, seek their revenge."

"I hope you're right," Marina said, her eyes on his tortured face, and she meant it because her love was big enough at that moment to want him to have what was best for him even if it did not include herself.

He kissed her tenderly.

"Take care of yourself, my darling," he said. "If anything really frightening occurs, send one of the children to find me. They'll know where Handrathi

187

will be, but whatever you do, don't come yourself. You somehow don't look as though you belonged to this set-up, not even in your pretty dress."

Then smiling into his eyes and because she could not resist him she put her arms round his neck and drew his face to hers.

"I love you, I love you," she heard herself saying and she was still repeating the words as he slipped from her arms and out through the caravan door, shutting it firmly behind him.

Marina washed up the tea cups and then a knock at the door made her start apprehensively.

"Are you there, luv?"

It was the gypsy woman from the adjacent caravan. Marina opened the door.

"Oh, you do look nice!" the woman exclaimed, staring at the coloured skirt. "I saw that in Ma Johnson's, but I couldn't afford it, not this week. I 'ad to buy a new washing bowl—the old one 'ad a 'uge 'ole in it."

"I expect Mrs Johnson will have other skirts just as pretty," Marina said consolingly.

"Oh, I dare say I'll find something in one of the markets," the woman answered. "That old skinflint puts far too much on her goods. I buy if I'm pressed or if I want credit; but if I pay cash there's lots of places cheaper and that's the truth."

"I hear we're moving tonight," Marina said to change the subject.

"That's what I came to see you about," the gypsy woman said. "Mind you put everything careful so it can't fall down. These caravans sway something awful when we're on the move. Coming here I broke half a dozen plates."

"I'm glad you told me," Marina said.

"Put things on the bed, that's the safest," the woman advised her. "So long, luv."

She moved back to her own caravan.

Marina did as had been suggested, packing her newly bought plates and cups on the bed and covering them with a blanket. Surely, she thought with a little smile, the effort was hardly worth it. Soon, perhaps tomorrow, she and Carlos would be flitting away and leaving all this behind.

She made up her mind to attach a note to her coloured skirt saying it was for the woman next door as a reward for being kind and friendly. The thought of it reminded her of her clothes and Carlos's.

She set to work rather inexpertly to wash Carlos's shirt and her blouse and her under-clothes. At first she was not very successful. The clothes looked patchy with lumps of soap-flakes stuck in them, but after two or three rinses they appeared to be clean.

She wrung them out and hung them over the sink wishing she had done it earlier in the day when they could have dried in the sunshine.

By the time she had finished it was growing dusk. The sound of the merry-go-round came tinkling to her ears and above it she could occasionally hear the clapping and cheers from the audience in the big tent.

They must be making money tonight, she thought and suddenly realised it was Saturday. The days had gone by so quickly she hadn't the time to remember the days of the week.

What would Sybil be doing? she wondered. Poor Sybil! Was she hoping vainly to hear from Lisbon that her employer had arrived safely? Marina wondered what Sybil or any of her friends would think if they could see her now.

As she thought of them she realised that, perhaps

189

with the exception of Sybil, not one of them would understand. She could almost hear them laughing and sniggering over the whole episode:

"Fancy, my dear, Marina caught up with some South American adventurer and dragged all over Europe. She even stayed with him in a gypsy caravan!"

She could imagine the look in their eyes. The manner in which they would mouth over the news, quite convinced that she was living with Carlos and not thinking that her love for him could be anything but a wild infatuation.

"How Marina could find that sort of person amusing I don't know!" The more staid of her acquaintances would put it that way, while others would say: "Oh, darling, those South Americans are so fascinating for a time."

She looked round the tiny caravan, at the bed where she and Carlos had lain this afternoon and where she had come so very near to surrendering herself completely to him.

He didn't love her enough, and yet she was happier than she had ever been in her life before. She knew that none of the people she had ever known who had played a part in her life were of the least importance—they were just shadows. She had never been alive till this moment! If she and Carlos died tonight, he had given her that—a few days in which she had known the full ecstasy of living.

She saw the curtains Ma Johnson had lent her lying on the floor where Carlos had thrown them. She picked them up automatically but made no attempt to hang them. Somehow they didn't seem important any more.

It was Carlos she wanted to think about, to remember and to dream about, almost as though he had already left her and she had only her memories of him.

She lay down on the bed on which she had not stacked the china and watched the light from outside making a pattern on the opposite wall. She felt as though she was in a little island with a wide expanse of water barring her from the mainland.

No one knew who she was. It was a strange, yet satisfactory feeling, and one thing she knew irrefutably and without argument was that all she wanted of life was to be Carlos's wife.

She must have dozed a little, for suddenly she was wakened by a lot of noise outside; the sound of engines, people shouting instructions, children's shrill voices screaming at each other and, in the distance, the roar of the caged animals.

Marina jumped to her feet and as she did so there was a sharp rapping at her door. She hurried to open it and saw outside, grinning at her in the light from a motor-car's head lamp, the impudent face of Jimmy.

"Ready?" he asked.

"Oh, are we going now?" Marina questioned in surprise.

"We're starting in a few minutes," he answered.

He looked towards the circus as he spoke and Marina saw that the big tent was coming down and that the merry-go-round, which was now silent, was being dismantled.

"Your husband'll be busy," he said, "so I'll look after you."

"You mean you're going to pull the caravan?" Marina asked looking at the motor which he had drawn up at the side of the van, its engine still running.

"That's right," he replied. "I hope you feel honoured."

"What about your own caravan?" Marina enquired.

"It's all arranged," he replied. "Get a coat or something and come and sit beside me in the car."

"I think perhaps I'd better stay in the caravan," Marina told him, seeing the look in his eyes.

"Don't be a fool," he answered, "you'll be sick as a cat. Besides I want to have a talk with you."

Marina looked at him a little helplessly. There was something forceful about him and she guessed she was likely to have trouble on the journey if Master Jim was her companion; but at the same time there didn't seem to be much alternative. Carlos was working and she couldn't very well ask one of the women from one of the other caravans to chaperone her.

"Oh, well," she thought; she was used to taking care of herself and she didn't suppose that Jim was very much different from the playboys and young men of Mayfair, who'd tried ever since she grew up to seduce her one way or another. If they hadn't wanted to marry her, they had wanted to go to bed with her.

She had grown quite adept at saying "No", but it was only because of the unusual circumstances in which she found herself that she felt at all nervous about being alone with Jim. At least he'd be driving, which would be one blessing.

"I'll get a coat," she said.

She went back into the caravan, picked up her handbag and her white dressing case: she didn't intend to be separated from that. She put in it her face creams, powder and all the things she had brought with her from Lisbon. It wouldn't do to leave them lying about; they all looked too expensive for the wife of a circus hand.

She opened the cupboard and took out the cardigan she had bought from Mrs Johnson that morning; her coat and skirt and Carlos's suit were hanging there and she remembered guiltily she hadn't pressed them as she had said she would.

She threw the cardigan over her shoulders, found a silk handerchief and tied it over her head; she was rather sorry she was wearing the cheap but pretty blouse and gypsy skirt she had bought from Ma Johnson.

She felt that her more severely-cut suit would be likely to have a more restraining effect on Master Jim. Then she smiled a little ruefully at herself—nothing, she was certain, would restrain Jim. He was that type.

She had met him before in a more educated form and she knew exactly what he was like.

There were bumps and bangs, she was nearly thrown off her feet as the caravan moved about apparently being connected to Jim's car. Then she heard him give a shout and, picking up her things, she hurried outside.

The caravans were all on the move being trundled along behind cars, trucks and lorries in the long queue.

The big tent had now disappeared and was being stacked up by dozens of men whom Marina could see working with flood lights trained on them. She tried to recognise Carlos but failed, and remembered he would be looking after the horses.

"Come on," Jim called.

The car was large and had doubtless once been expensive. The front seat was roomy and comfortable and she scrambled in and pulled down the arm rest between them. He turned round to face her; the engine was running but they were not on the move.

"Why the barricade?" he asked.

"You know the answer to that one," Marina retorted.

"You know I like you," Jim smiled. "I like your spirit. I think we're going to get along well together."

"We will, if you behave yourself," Marina said, "If not, I shall get out and walk."

"You're that type of girl, are you?" Jim asked, his grin stretching from ear to ear.

"Yes, I am," Marina answered. "We might as well make things clear from the beginning."

"You'll change your mind," Jim told her. "They all do, you know."

"How boring for you!" Marina answered.

"What d'you mean by that?"

It was obvious that the conversation was not going entirely according to plan.

"Nothing that's easy is worth having," Marina said, "you should know that."

"That might be true, and again it might not," Jim said evasively. "C'mon, be nice to me. I've had a hell of a row with Ma because I said I was going to pull your caravan rather than hers."

"You ought to be ashamed of yourself," Marina retorted; "of course she was annoyed. Then, what about me? You're getting me talked about. Think of what all the others will say."

"D'you think I care?" Jim asked. "I've been thinking about you all day. You're a real eyeful. We don't often get them as pretty as you in this dump."

"Thanks for the compliment," Marina said, "but what I think you really ought to do is to tell your mother you've changed your mind."

"Oh, stow it," Jim said sourly. "I'm not going to listen to arguments all over again and she ain't my mother. Can't think why the Old Man married her. She nags the head off 'im."

"Why don't you get married and stop running after other people's wives?" Marina asked.

Jim threw back his head and laughed.

"You pack a clean punch, don't you?" he asked. "Maybe you'll find the answer to that question before the journey's over. Here! It looks as though we're moving. The Old Man's been speeding up things tonight. He always gets impatient to get on to the next place. He always believes there'll be more money in it. You know the idea—jam tomorrow but never jam today."

"How were you educated?" Marina asked.

He looked astonished as though it was the last question he expected.

"As a matter of fact, the Old Man was rather strict about it," he said. "It was during the war and of course the Circus was disbanded, the big tent stored away. It nearly broke his heart, it did, but it was me who suffered from it. He had me working at my lessons till I thought I'd go mad. I not only had to go to school.

"I had to have extra classes, 'tutors'—don't make me laugh. People in our class don't have tutors, but the Old Man found them; retired school masters and the like. They worked with me in the evening. You never saw such a set-to!

"There were we living on half a potato—he didn't want to touch his savings not more than he could help and money being poured out on my education. It makes me laugh to think of it."

"You should be grateful instead of sneering at your father," Marina said. "I knew at once you had been better educated than the average man in your position."

"Does that make me seem more attractive to you?" Jim enquired. "If it did, it would all have been worthwhile. No other woman's been interested in all that learning that was stuffed into my head."

"Don't you understand what an asset it is?" Marina asked. "Not to make you more attractive to some stupid woman, but so that you can earn more, be more successful, be more important if you like."

"Well, I'm damned!" he ejaculated. "I was wondering this afternoon what we'd talk about when we were alone here in the car, but I never expected it to be about my education."

"You'll find out I'm right," Marina said. "One day you might even write a book about the Circus, but in the meantime, you could use your intelligence to improve some of the acts."

"What d'you know about them?" Jim asked. "I don't believe you've even seen them. You only arrived last night."

"I've seen big circuses," Marina answered. "I've seen them in England and in . . ."

She was just going to say she had seen them in New York and changed her mind.

"I know what the turns are like," she went on hurriedly, "They're not good enough. Your father may be satisfied with them, but you could think of something better."

"What I want is somebody like you to help me," Jim said. "You see, a clever woman can make anything of a man. I know you seem to think I have possibilities. What are you going to do about that?"

As he spoke his left arm reached out along the seat behind Marina. She could feel the pressure of it against her shoulders. "Oh dear," she thought with a little sigh, "this is going to be a very difficult journey."

10

The long procession of trucks and caravans and cages began to move very slowly off into the darkness.

Marina, because she was anxious to talk about anything that was not intimate, asked Jim about the arrangements they made and how it was possible to move so many people, tents and fair material, so quickly.

"The Old Man's been doing it for years," he replied. "There's not much money in it and when he is dead I doubt if I shall keep the Circus going."

"It'd be a pity to close it," Marina said.

"I think I'd rather take a few of the acts round the music halls," Jim answered, then added: "All the same, the wanderlust is in my blood! I dare say I shall keep on, especially if I can find a nice bit of skirt to keep me interested in it."

Marina did not answer, and after a moment, obviously following a train of thought, he said:

"What made you marry that South American guy?"

"I loved him," Marina answered.

"I never did think much of those dagos," Jim said scornfully. "We've employed a lot of them one way and another; they're always shifty. For all you know, that man of yours may have half a dozen wives back home."

"Not everyone's crooked," she said in what she hoped was a crushing tone, but Jim only laughed.

"Meaning that I am, I suppose," he said with a

sidelong glance at her. "Well, if it comes to that, I do steal pretty women."

"I think your mind runs too much on the opposite sex," Marina told him. "Why don't you do a bit of hard work and try to improve the Circus? Carlos said you've got some good material there."

"What the hell does Carlos know about it?" Jim asked almost angrily. "Neither you nor he are circus folk and well you know it. If the Old Man hadn't been short-handed he'd never have taken you on."

"But he did," Marina retorted; "and Carlos is very good with horses. If you don't believe me, ask Mr. Handrathi."

"Handrathi's opinions don't interest me one way or another," Jim said sharply.

There had obviously been a disagreement here, because after a moment he changed the subject and said in a very different tone:

"Tell me about yourself. Where do you come from in England?"

"London," Marina answered.

"That's very explicit, I must say; that tells me a real lot, that does."

"Well, I'm not really interested in talking about myself to strangers," Marina answered. "Tell me about the Circus."

"I'm not really interested in talking about the Circus to strangers," Jim said mimicking her tone.

Marina was silent thinking this was obviously going to be a very uncomfortable trip; then, suddenly, Jim's arm went around her and he pulled her close beside him before she was aware what was happening.

"Let's stow the talk," he said roughly. "I think you're the prettiest bit of goods I've seen for a long time. We'll have a bit of fun together. These night

198

journeys are usually damn boring, but this one needn't be."

Marina pushed him away with all her strength.

"Don't you dare touch me," she said. "If you do that again, I shall go and sit in the caravan behind. I shouldn't have come with you in the first place."

"Hoity toity!" he answered, his arm still round her but released a little so that she was not squeezed against him.

"Let me go, please," Marina said in a cold icy voice which had always been effective in the past in dealing with the young men who grew too familiar.

"What's biting you?" he asked; but at that moment the carvan in front of them came to a sudden stop. Jim was forced to take his arm away while he jammed on the brake, and Marina was free.

She grabbed the door handle and opened it:

"Am I going behind?" she asked, "or are you going to behave?"

Jim took his hand from the wheel and turned round to face her:

"God, you're pretty!" he exclaimed. "I thought you were smashing when I first saw you. In that blouse and coloured skirt you make quite a picture. Don't be beastly to me."

He was coarse and vulgar, but Marina had to admit it, he did have a certain amount of charm. Yet something warned her that he was not a person to be trifled with.

"Listen," she said, "we're at a standstill and I can easily get into my own caravan, and unless you give me your word of honour that you'll behave like a gentleman, I'm not going to stay with you. You can drive alone."

"Don't you like me a little bit?" he asked.

"That's not the point," Marina said. "I'm not going

to be mauled about and you've got to swear you won't touch me again."

Jim saw that she was serious. The caravan in front started to move on, and he made up his mind.

"O.K.—have it your own way, but I must say I'm disappointed in you."

"That's too bad, isn't it?" Marina commented.

"Married or single, what's the difference?" Jim asked. "Besides, if it comes to that, it's usually the married ones that're more ready for it."

"Then you have made a mistake in this instance," Marina said firmly. "I love my husband and I'm not in the least interested in anyone else. Have I made myself clear?"

"Too damn' clear," Jim answered. "I'd like to know who you think you are, giving yourself airs and setting yourself up as a kind of purity league. But you'll change! They all do after a time. It's just bad luck meeting you so soon after your marriage."

"You've got a pretty poor opinion of women, haven't you?" Marina asked.

"Women are for loving," Jim replied.

"And yet you've never married?" Marina queried.

"I've seen too much of married women to put my head in a noose," Jim chuckled. "I grant you I may have met the wrong sort, but if I'd met a girl like you things would've been different."

"That's good sales talk," Marina flashed. "You said it too glibly for it to sound sincere."

"Critical—that's what you're being."

He turned to grin at her and then looked back to the road.

"No, you're different," he said perceptively. "There's something about you I can't put my finger on. You look sexy but when it comes down to brass tacks you behave like a bloomin' refrigerator."

"That's how I feel towards everyone except Carlos," Marina said truthfully.

"What's this Carlos fellow got that I haven't?" Jim asked.

His question set off a train of thought in Marina's mind. What was it about Carlos that attracted her so greatly? She had known so many men in her life, men who had loved her to distraction, men like Victor who seemed completely and utterly suitable and yet had not sparked off the right response as far as she was concerned.

Where was Carlos different? He was good looking, but so were hundreds of others. He had charm, good manners and a kind of authority which she found attractive but which might have repulsed other people. Perhaps, she thought, it was the manliness about him. He had a toughness which she had missed in so many men who had courted her, while his manners were impeccable.

There was nothing rough about him even though she knew that if he gave an order he expected it to be obeyed. Yet all these things added up to nothing of any real consequence.

What did matter was the fact that he had only to touch her to set her on fire. She had only to feel him close to her to know that she longed for his arms round her, his lips on hers.

She shut her eyes for a moment and she could feel the ecstasy and the joy sweeping over her. She remembered again that moment when they had lain together on the narrow bed and she had so nearly surrendered herself to him.

She had wanted him at that moment with an overwhelming desire which was stronger than anything she had ever known, stronger than she had ever envisaged. It was only by a miracle, a force of will she had not known she possessed, that she had torn herself free and had refused him what he wanted.

"I love him," she thought now, "and yet I could say No."

She wondered how she could have been so strong; and then she knew that her love for Carlos was the finest, the most splendid thing in her whole life, and she dare not debase it, dare not soil it in any way for fear it should vanish.

This was something sacred, almost holy. She could not bear the bond between them not to be as perfect as the ideal love she had been seeking all her life.

Jim's voice broke in on her thoughts.

"What're you thinking about?" he asked.

"It's a secret," Marina answered.

"Then I guess it's about me," he said conceitedly.

"In which case you guess wrong," Marina answered. "As a matter of fact I was thinking about my husband, wondering how he is getting on with the horses. Do they travel in front or behind the rest?"

"What the hell does it matter?" Jim said roughly. "You're a bore about your man, that's what you are. What's he do to you—whip you to make you so submissive?"

Marina did not answer and he laughed.

"I bet that's the truth. Women are like animals. You've got to tame them. If you cosset them, they turn away; crack the whip and they fall at your feet."

"That's quite untrue," Marina said. "You treat women as playthings and they're nothing of the sort, and because of your attitude you'll never meet the right sort of woman."

"How d'you know I haven't met her already?" Jim asked with a sidelong glance. "You intrigue me. You look pretty and dumb, but you've got a brain, I'll say that for you."

"Thank you," Marina said sarcastically. "I appreciate the compliment."

"I don't like brains in women as a rule," Jim went on. "Too much talk gets you nowhere. Talk is for men: women should be soft and willing."

"Only where you're concerned!" Marina retorted. "You know, it's a strange thing but there are other men in the world. Men with not such degrading ideas."

"Now see here," Jim said, "you can talk all you like, but what's the life of an average woman. She's pretty for a few years and if she's got any sense she'll make the most of them and have a bit of fun because for the rest of her life she's just going to slave away with a lot of kids and a husband who's on the lookout for a bird who looks like she did when she was young."

"Stop! Don't say it; you frighten me!" Marina said. "It horrifies me that anyone should have such low ideas of me and my whole sex."

"You don't like the truth, that's all," Jim smiled. "I don't suppose, if it comes to that, you ever hear it. You're at the pretty stage; some men will tell you that you're what they've been looking for all their lives and all that sort of stuff. Once they've had what they want, what happens? They go off to find someone else."

He paused and after a moment added, almost defiantly:

"That's the truth, isn't it?"

Marina was thinking of her friends. In some horrible way part of what he said was true. She remembered the liaisons among those she knew in London, Paris and New York. She remembered a friend of hers who had lost her husband to another woman saying, with the tears pouring down her face,

"He couldn't get me without marriage, so he married me. Now he is looking for someone else who is hard to get!"

Marina shivered. Was that all life held for her? A husband who wanted her when she was young and attractive and who, when she was old, would be unfaithful with younger women.

"That's made you think, hasn't it?" Jim asked jeeringly.

"Be quiet!" she stormed at him. "You're upsetting me and making me unhappy."

She was answering her own thoughts rather than Jim, but it left him quite unperturbed.

"I tell you, kisses are better than talk," he said. "You never get anywhere with words. Let's try kissing for a change."

He put out his arm as he spoke, but Marina shrank away from him.

"You promised," she said warningly.

"If you get out now, you'll break a leg," he warned.

They were moving more swiftly because now they were on the highway.

"How far are we going?" Marina asked.

"Outside Lebrune," he answered. "It's a good pitch. If the weather's fine we shall be packing them in for the afternoon performance."

"What do you do when we arrive?" Marina said.

"The men put up the big tent and the rest of the paraphernalia. Worried about your husband? He'll be too busy and too tired to attend to you, I can promise you that."

"I was only wondering," Marina said. "It seems pretty exhausting, to travel all night and start a performance right away."

"Most of them expect their wages on Friday night, don't forget that," Jim said.

204

"You don't seem to be doing much work for yours," Marina told him.

"That's all you know," Jim retorted. "Somebody has to do a bit of overseeing, otherwise they'd slack off and the whole thing would be a flop. The Old Man has come to rely on me." He paused and added: "What I says goes; just remember that if you want your dear little husband to keep his job."

"Don't say you are trying to blackmail me," Marina exclaimed. "That really would be the last straw."

There was laughter in her voice and she spoke lightly; at the same time she knew Jim might in all seriousness carry out his threat.

"Blackmail is an unpleasant word," he answered; "but supposing your husband wanted a nice rise and perhaps a better place to park his caravan—there's quite a lot of difference in being the far side of the ground or right up against the music of the hurdy-gurdy."

He turned to look at Marina's face.

"You like your comfort, don't you? What girl doesn't?" he asked. "And sometimes the pretty ones are short of money. Oh, there's lots of things your Uncle Jim can do for him if you keep on the right side of him."

"I still say it's blackmail," Marina said clearly. "And, quite frankly, your sharp sales talk doesn't impress me."

"It's a pity," Jim said. "You wouldn't like your poor dear hubby to have all the worst jobs to do, would you? Some are better than others and some are even quite dangerous."

It was Marina this time who turned round in her seat to look at him.

"You really are a cad, aren't you?" she said. "Haven't you any sense of integrity or decency?"

"None where women are concerned," he said cheerily; "and I've told you I think you're damned pretty—and I'm going all-out to get you. Have I made myself clear?"

"You're talking a lot of nonsense," Marina said defiantly. "Do I have to tell you again that I haven't been married long? I love my husband and I shall never look at any other man—especially you."

Jim laughed.

"We'll see," he said. "In the meantime, don't blame me if he doesn't like what's coming to him."

There was somehow a threat behind the words which made Marina feel uncomfortable. She did not reply and did not look at Jim. She had the feeling it would be unwise to go too far with this conversation.

It was obvious that he was utterly unscrupulous and some instinct warned her that the more elusive she appeared the more insistent he would become.

Jim Johnson was obviously used to having his own way. His direct approach to what he wanted, the fact that he was the Boss's son, and because he did not scruple to use any means to gain his ends, must have brought him a great deal of success with a certain type of woman.

It would be hard to convince him that she was not like the others, and somehow, although she told herself it was nonsense, she had the feeling that he might take out on Carlos his disappointment and feeling of frustration.

"How much longer before we get there?" Marina asked, trying to change the subject.

Jim glanced at the flashy watch on a wide silver bracelet he wore on his sunburnt arm.

"Another hour!" he answered. "Come a bit closer. I've got something I want to tell you."

"I'm quite all right," Marina answered. "Besides you promised. Had you forgotten that?"

"You're not likely to let me forget it," he growled. "Why are you so choosey? A few kisses never hurt anyone."

"The answer to that question is that I don't like kissing strange people," Marina replied.

"I'm no stranger," Jim said. "Why, you've known me quite a long time by now. Remember how I carried your things down from Ma's to your caravan? That was pretty decent of me, wasn't it? If you weren't so pretty, I'd have sent one of the gypsy boys."

"I was quite prepared to tip you," Marina said.

He laughed.

"I like that touch," he said. "You ought to have seen your face when I told you it wasn't the sort of tip I wanted. Where have you been all these years? Shut up in a convent, or something? You don't seem to know anything."

Marina might have replied she wasn't in the habit of meeting men who brought parcels to the door and if she had she wouldn't have thought of them in terms of being prospective suitors or men who would like to kiss her.

She wondered if Jim would ever appreciate the gulf that lay between them; the gulf of position, education, money; and then she told herself severely that none of these things mattered at the moment. She and Jim were just a man and a woman alone in a slowly moving car and it didn't really matter what they possessed or who they were. She was just a woman with sex appeal and he was a man who desired her.

For a moment she felt almost sorry for him. He missed so much of life. Then surprisingly she found herself asking the question as to whether this healthy, frank approach to the business of living was not, in its way, better than her superficial, sophisticated one.

"Tell me, Jim," she said, "what do you really want of life? What's your ambition?"

"To make love to you," he answered.

"No, no," she said quickly; "not the obvious answer, not something transitory, happening at this moment. I'm asking your ambitions, your aspirations. What do you look forward to?"

"Money and women," he answered with a grin, "and a lot of good drink thrown in. What else is there, if it comes to that?"

Marina couldn't help laughing. She had asked the question, she had got the answer, and when it came to brass tacks, what else was there?

She doubted if Jim had ever read a book since he left school. Any information about current affairs would come from the wireless, not from the newspapers; and she was certain that he had in fact spoken the truth when he said what he wanted was money and women.

She thought of Victor. Hadn't Victor wanted the same things. He made no particular search for money; he had so much. But women were certainly his interest apart from a few superficial other methods by which he passed the time—racing, travelling, gambling.

They were all part of his life. But his main interest for the past year at any rate, had been the pursuit of her.

"Am I condemning Jim unfairly," she asked herself, "merely because he is of a different class?"

"Now what are you thinking about?" Jim enquired, "and if you're thinking up any more questions for me, you can answer them yourself. What

I want is a bit of comfort. Come and sit close to me. Stop thinking you're a nun or something and be a little human."

"I can be 'a little human' without sitting close to you," Marina answered.

"In other words, you can go on talking," Jim said wearily. "God! but I'm sorry for that husband of yours. Do you keep him up half the night lecturing him when all he wants is to get to bed with a nice soft bit of flesh."

"Being married is very different from what you are suggesting," Marina said. "Get yourself a wife and you'll cease to be a menace."

"So that's what you think I am?" he asked. "Well, there's other people who have other words for it, I can promise you that. There's not many as have said they were not satisfied. And the answer to that, in case you are thinking of one, is you can't pass an opinion on something you haven't sampled."

Marina couldn't help laughing.

"You're incorrigible," she said. "I believe we might even be friends if you would behave decently and keep your hands to yourself."

"It's wonderful, isn't it," Jim said addressing himself to the road ahead. "Here I meet a girl who really attracts me, who's really got something, and she offers to be friends. I must be slipping."

"You might be growing up," Marina said.

"Oh, you've got an answer to everything," he said. "Too sharp by half, that's what you are."

As he spoke the caravan in front slowed down a little. Marina opened the window and looked out.

"I can see houses," she said. "We must be getting near the town."

"We can't be far off," Jim agreed. "I suppose I should thank you. You've made the journey pass quite quickly—though it wasn't exactly what I'd expected."

"I always thought it dangerous to drive with one hand, any way," Marina said a little impishly.

"I always thought it was dangerous to play with fire and I've not finished by any means."

There was an underlying threat in the lightness of his tone and Marina, with a little shrug of her shoulders, told herself that tomorrow or the next day they might be moving on. She couldn't believe he was really serious in his threat where Carlos was concerned, and yet she felt uneasy.

She had noticed from the very first there was a ruthlessness about Jim which told her he was not the type of man to obey the laws of cricket.

She put her head out of the window again. Far ahead she could see the lights of vehicles turning left off the road.

"I think we must be going on to the field," she said; "how exciting! I shall look forward to seeing what it's like tomorrow."

"We've got a lot of work to do before daylight," Jim told her.

"Why don't you leave the putting up of the tent and all the other things until the morning?"

"It's not a good advertisement," he replied. "People come round quite early to see what's happening and if they see everything half-unpacked it looks sordid and not very exciting, so they don't come back and pay their money to get in. No, the Old Man's right in insisting everything goes up as soon as we arrive and the staff can sleep later."

Marina could see there was some point in that. She remembered once as a child seeing a Fair being dismantled and thinking how small the Big Wheel looked when it was in sections and how the horses

210

on the merry-go-round, which in movement had had a magic of their own, looked sad and dilapidated as the men heaved them one by one onto a lorry.

She could understand that there was a great deal of psychology in the arrangement of a circus, in getting the audience infected by the glamour and excitement of it long before they actually paid their money to go into the big tent.

Now, as they drew nearer and nearer the turning the others had taken, she could see caravans and lorries in the front making a great circle on a flat piece of waste ground.

There were houses in the distance instead of open country which had been there at the last stopping place, and she wondered if Carlos had found out anything about an air-field.

Tentatively choosing her words so that they should sound casual, she said:

"I've a feeling there's an air-field somewhere near here. I used to have a friend who was a ferry pilot and I remember him talking about Lebrune."

"One of your young men, was he?" he asked. "Did you let him make love to you?"

"Not in the way you mean," Marina answered.

"That means he did," Jim said positively. "I bet this husband of yours wasn't your first lover, was he?"

"Of course he was," Marina said almost angrily. "Why do you twist everything I say? I was asking you about the air-field."

"I'm not interested in air-fields—only in you," Jim answered. "Do you realise we have passed half the night together and you haven't told me a damned thing about yourself."

"You haven't told me much either," Marina retorted. "Only that you run after every pretty woman you meet."

"What's wrong with that?" he asked. "Stop chipping at a man. My God! You'll be a nagger when you're old."

"Luckily I shan't be a nuisance to you," she said jokingly.

She was still looking out of the window as she spoke. Suddenly she felt Jim's heavy hand on her shoulder. He jerked her across the seat till once again she was close to him.

"You're driving me up the wall," he said. "There's something about you—I don't know what it is—which makes me feel as I have never felt before for any woman. I want to kiss you and I want to make love to you and at the same time I want to beat you."

Marina hardly heard what he said as she was struggling to free herself.

"Let me go!" she cried. "You promised."

"I promised to behave until we arrived," he said. "If you want to get out and walk you can do so. You won't get far, I'll soon catch up with you."

There was something in his tone which told Marina he was speaking the truth.

"I'm not going to run away," she said. "Let me go!"

"Why should I?" he asked, holding her a little closer.

"Because I ask you to," she replied. "Because you're much stronger than I am. I won't fight against you."

"Damn it all, you can always make out an argument in your own favour, can't you?" Jim said.

He let her go, but as he did so Marina realised it was not because of what she had said, but because he needed both hands for turning the corner.

"A wasted drive," Jim said. "Well, you'll have to make up for it sometimes. Even people like you pay their debts."

"So I'm to consider myself in your debt," Marina said. "Granted you offered me a ride, but look how I've kept you amused; you've laughed quite a lot. Do you realise that?"

"You're a provocative little devil," Jim said. "And what's more, you know it. You've not seen the last of me, young lady."

Marina decided to ignore the threat and put her head out of the window.

"I can see the animal cages now," she said. "They're pulling up to the right."

"Then we'll go left," Jim said. "The Old Man hates to be on top of the lions; he says they keep him awake at night."

He moved out of the queue and they bumped across some rough uneven ground in a manner which made Marina glad she was not behind in the swinging, jerking caravan. It was like being in a very rough sea, she thought and remembered she never had been a good sailor.

Jim's headlights revealed that not far ahead of them was the red and white caravan which she knew belonged to his father. They followed at a discreet distance and when it came to a stop Jim parked two or three paces behind it.

"There," he said as they came to a standstill, "are you going to say 'Thank you'?"

"Of course I am," Marina answered. "Thank you very much."

"Oh, stow it," he said. "You know what I mean."

Because she knew exactly what he meant Marina hastily opened the door and scrambled out the other side of the car. Lifting her white cosmetics case and her handbag, she carried them to the door of the caravan and opened it.

The lights from the cars and lorries outside made it easy to see almost clearly and the ride didn't seem to have broken or upset anything inside the caravan. In fact everything seemed to be intact.

Marina put down her case. She realised suddenly that she was very tired. She could hear Jim uncoupling the caravan from the car and then she heard the noise of the engine and hoped he had moved off.

"I'll light the lantern and get the things off the bed," Marina thought, "and then when Carlos comes back he'll be able to go to sleep."

She pulled the blanket off Carlos's bed on which they had stacked the plates and at that moment she heard the caravan door open.

"Is that you, Carlos?" she called excitedly.

The leap of her heart told her how much she had been waiting for him.

"He won't be here for a long time yet," a voice replied, and Marina, holding a plate in her hand turned to see Jim.

Too late she realised she had been a fool not to lock the door. In the moving lights from outside she could see the expression on his face, the gleam in his eyes.

"Thank you so much for towing the caravan," she said, trying to speak in an unconcerned, easy manner. "It was sweet of you; but now, if you don't mind, I'm tired and I want to go to bed."

"I had the same idea," he answered and she didn't pretend to misunderstand him.

"Now, Jim, please don't be difficult," she said. "I really have had a long day and I've got to put all these plates away."

She held out the plate she was holding in her hand almost as if it was a shield between them. But, before she could say any more or even move, he was upon her.

He took the plate from her and chucked it on the floor. She heard it break, then she was fighting wildly, struggling like a captured animal against the strength of his arms.

His hands tried to caress her body and his mouth was trying to imprison hers. He was rough and brutal. She felt almost despairingly that her strength would not last long.

She fought, desperately pounding against his heavy chest with her clenched fists, attempting to scratch his face, kicking with both her feet as he lifted her off the ground; and she knew it was quite hopeless.

As he lifted her on to her own bed she gave a frightened cry:

"Please don't, don't," she managed to say breathlessly and with her voice choking in her throat; "don't, Jim, don't. Leave me alone."

"You have tempted me long enough," he said through clenched teeth, "you little tiger cat, I'll take you yet."

He threw himself down on top of her. She felt the breath go from her body and then his mouth was on hers silencing her protests and making her feel as though a sudden darkness had fallen upon her suffocating her almost into insensibility.

Suddenly, so unexpectedly, she could hardly believe it was true, she heard a voice say:

"My God!" Then: "Get up, you swine!"

Jim raised his head from her lips as someone towering over them yanked him to his feet.

For a moment, he seemed too astonished to speak

until a cracking blow on the side of his face brought him to his senses.

"Don't you hit me, you South American rat," he snarled.

The last word ended almost in a yell as Carlos caught him a quick punch to the stomach and another on the side of his chin. He staggered, but recovered and rushed like a bull at the smaller man, his arms seemingly immense flailing out like a windmill.

Marina gave a shriek of horror. She was certain Carlos would be killed. Carlos who was so much smaller than this great rough giant of a man. But in the shifting light coming in through the window she saw Carlos side-step Jim's blow and, at the same time, catch him a terrific upper-cut on the point of his chin.

Jim staggered backwards, and Marina screamed again because she thought he was about to fall on her, but he missed the bed, crumpled to the floor and hit his head as he did so a terrific crack against the side of the caravan. His fall rocked the fragile structure, and then there was silence.

Marina could see him sprawled and apparently unconscious. Carlos looked down at him.

"Get me some rope," he said sharply, "and that silk handkerchief you wear round your head."

"What're you going to do?" Marina asked, her voice sounding like a thin croak from between her bruised lips; but almost automatically because of the command in Carlos's voice she obeyed him.

There wasn't such a thing as rope in the caravan, she thought wildly until she remembered the curtains which Mrs Johnson had lent her were attached to a long piece of cord.

"Hurry up," Carlos called sharply, and she was afraid of his tone.

"This is the only thing we have," she said piteously, holding out the curtains.

He took them from her without a word and pulled the rings off the cord. She watched him with surprise as he turned Jim over and tied his hands behind his back. She could see the thin cord cutting into the brown flesh below his wrist watch, but she said nothing, only watched.

"Fetch the other curtain," Carlos said over his shoulder.

Marina obeyed him. Again he pulled the cord free through the brightly coloured curtain, knelt on the floor and tied Jim's legs together.

"Your handkerchief," he said briefly.

For a moment she could not remember where it was, and then recalled that she had it over her head during the whole journey; now owing to Jim's embrace it had slipped back from her hair and was hanging down her back, the knot resting against her throat.

She undid it and gave it to Carlos. She watched him force it between Jim's teeth and tie it tightly behind his head.

"What are you doing?" she asked in a whisper. "There'll be trouble if you treat him like this—you know there will."

"We shan't be here to see it: we're going."

"Going," Marina repeated stupidly, "but where to?"

"Out of here," Carlos answered. "Come on. We must get away while everybody's busy."

"But Carlos, we can't go like this," Marina said looking down at her crumpled skirt.

Jim had torn the cheap blouse at the neck and

217

almost instinctively her fingers went up to hide the tear from Carlos.

"We're going as we are," he said. "Take some things over your arm, if you like, but we've got to get away."

Marina realised there was no time to waste. Going to the cupboard she dragged out her own suit and Carlos's, finding them by feel for it was too dark for her to see. His shirt and her blouse were hanging over the sink. She pulled them down and then, remembering she had been wearing a cardigan, walked across the caravan and reached over the recumbent Jim to take it from the bed.

"Come on," Carlos said impatiently.

She picked up her white vanity case and her handbag and came behind him where he stood at the caravan door. He was looking out to where the others were moving.

The caravans were still coming in from the road. She could see them bumping over the rough ground towards where the tractors and cages had come to rest, and she could hear raised voices as someone shouted instructions.

"Come on," Carlos said.

He turned to take her case from her, then stepped out on to the ground and went behind the caravan. She followed him, holding the bundle of clothes and feeling bewildered and a little frightened.

What would happen when Jim became conscious again? He had taken a heavy crack on the head as well as Carlos's knock-out blow on the chin. But she was certain that he was too strong and tough for that to render him unconscious for very long.

Carlos reached out and took her free hand in his. He was walking quickly and she had difficulty in keeping up with him. She stumbled over a tussock on the ground.

"Where are we going?" she asked.

"We're getting away from that lecher," he replied.

"Oh, Carlos, thank heaven you came in time," she said breathlessly, and aware that her voice sounded hoarse and frightened.

"What the hell were you doing with a man like that?" Carlos asked angrily.

She was too surprised to answer coherently.

"He came . . . he . . . he towed the caravan," she stammered. "What could I do?"

"You could have fetched me or gone with one of the other women," Carlos said, still in that tone of anger and irritation which made her feel as though she wanted to cry.

"I thought I could handle him," she said.

"You thought!" he said. "You know what sort of a man he is."

"I didn't," she answered.

They had reached the road and Carlos turned towards the town still walking very quickly.

"I've heard a good deal about Jim Johnson," Carlos said furiously. "Handrathi told me what he was like where women are concerned and when he wanted to get rid of a husband he got a gang to beat the man up. He has gone pretty close to murder on one or two occasions. I heard all that, but I didn't believe you were such a fool as to accept his company or let him into the caravan."

Marina stopped to try and get her breath.

"You're going too fast," she panted. "I can't keep up . . . please don't be angry with me . . . it wasn't my fault . . . I didn't know he was like that . . . you just went off and left me."

"Handrathi told me that one of the older hands
219

would be towing your caravan," Carlos answered. "It was only when we got here someone saw you driving across the field and said they expected Jim had had a pleasant drive."

"I'm grateful they did see us," Marina said. "If you hadn't come when you did—"

She stopped suddenly realising the full horror of what she had been through.

"Oh Carlos!" she said.

In answer he dragged her along the road regardless of the fact that her legs felt as though they could hardly carry her.

"We've got to get out of here," he said. "Jim Johnson is not going to take this lying down. Besides, if he has once made up his mind to get a woman, they say he always succeeds."

Because she was frightened Marina quickened her pace.

"I'm sorry, Carlos. It really wasn't my fault," she said again almost piteously.

"Now we no longer have the protection of the Circus," Carlos went on, "it may be dangerous for us in other ways."

"Dangerous?"

"Yes, there's always danger," he said angrily, "especially when one gets involved with a woman."

His tone of voice seemed to Marina to be the last straw.

She felt the tears gush into her eyes and flow down her cheeks. What she had already suffered at Jim's hands was bad enough, but it was nothing to the fact that Carlos was angry with her; angry, she thought despairingly, and regretting that he had ever loved her.

11

They walked for about a quarter of a mile in silence, Marina carrying the pile of clothing over her left arm and Carlos with her white vanity case in his hand. It was dark and more than once Marina stumbled, but he made no effort to assist her even although he had a free arm.

Quite suddenly she could bear the tension no longer.

"Darling, I'm sorry," she said. "Don't be angry with me, I can't bear it."

Her voice choked on the last words, and because her misery possessed her to such an extent, she could think of nothing else to say at this moment to Carlos in his anger.

A tiny, detached, mocking voice at the back of her brain asked, "Can this really be Marina Martyn speaking?"

Just for a moment she saw herself abject and humble because she was in love, and then even her critical faculty was lost and she said, her voice tremulous and shaken:

"Please, please answer me. I can't bear the silence."

"I'm silent," Carlos answered, "because I am ashamed."

He put his arm round her waist and drew her close beside him, at the same time they kept walking.

"How can you allow me to be so bestial to you, when you have been so wonderful?" he asked.

His voice was shaking almost as much as hers and she looked up at him, trying, in the moonlight coming between the clouds, to see the expression on his face.

"You're not angry?" she asked; her relief was inexpressible.

"I'm furious," he replied, his arm tightening around her. "When I came into the caravan and saw what the swine was doing, I wanted to kill him. I would have killed him if I'd had a weapon in my hands; and then, when we got away and we were alone, I think I hated you because you can make me feel so angry, because of the very intensity of my love."

Marina listened with her heart singing with thankfulness. As he spoke in a voice that vibrated with sincerity, she knew that such an explanation would have been impossible from an Englishman; even for Carlos it had been hard to say.

Just for an instant she leant her head against his shoulder.

"Oh, darling, I love you so much."

The words which she had said so often before were unimportant: it was the feeling behind them, the relief and above all the knowledge that Carlos loved her too which made her feel as though it was the first time they had passed her lips.

Carlos glanced over his shoulder.

"Come on; we must hurry," he said.

"You don't think Jim will follow us, do you?" Marina asked.

"I don't know," he answered. "I only know I want to get away from here. We'll make for the Airport; someone will be able to tell us where it is."

By now they had entered the town. The streets were deserted and there wasn't even a gendarme or a late night reveller to tell them the way. The street lamps replaced the moon to guide them and their feet seemed to echo on the pavements as they walked on and on, hoping they would see someone who could assist them.

"The Aerodrome might be this side of the town," Marina hazarded at length. From the pace they were moving her legs were tired and the bundle of clothes over her arm seemed to get heavier every minute.

"No, I think we're going in the right direction," Carlos answered. "I made some vague enquiries and I gathered from what I heard it was south of the town."

"I wonder how far outside," Marina asked.

"There must be someone about somewhere," Carlos said almost under his breath.

As he spoke they heard the noise of a car approaching from behind them. They both turned their heads and saw a long way down the road by which they had come, the headlights of a car.

"Perhaps we could get a lift," Marina said not very hopefully, but even as she spoke she realized that the car was doing a strange thing. It was zig-zagging from one side of the road to the other, its headlights full on.

"Must be a drunken driver," she said in tones almost of amusement before Carlos could speak, and then his hand was under her arm and he was pulling her swiftly down the street.

"What's the matter? Where're we going?" breathlessly she asked, surprised at his sudden increase of pace.

He didn't answer and then, ahead to the left of

them, she saw there was a church, a tall and ancient building with a pillared porch standing only a few paces back from the pavement.

Carlos turned and pulled her rapidly into the shadow of some Gothic pillars.

"What are you doing?" Marina asked. "I don't understand."

"I'm taking no chances," he answered.

The car was still coming down the road; it must have been moving very slowly, still zigzagging from side to side now it was approaching the street lights. It stopped and then went forward faster, the headlights still blazing.

The porch was not a deep one and Marina felt Carlos press her back against the wall and almost cover her body with his.

"Do you think it might be . . . ?" she began, only to hear him hush her into silence.

The car was drawing nearer, still moving very slowly, not more than fifteen miles an hour and then, peeping between the stone pillars, Marina could see the two men in the front and one man behind.

The man nearest to them, who was driving, was Jim. She could see his profile all too clearly and then she realised that the man behind him was hanging out of the car window and the man on the other side of Jim was doing the same thing.

They were scanning the houses as they passed, the alleyways opening out of them, the small gardens where there were bushes and trees, and Marina knew with a little throb of fear for whom they were looking.

Instinctively she raised the clothes she had on her arm up high against her face to hide the paleness of her blouse and her own neck and chin, only her eyes peeped out, dark and frightened; and then with a kind of sick horror which was beyond words she heard the car grind to a standstill.

"There's a church here," she heard the man behind Jim say. "We'll have a look inside."

Jim turned his face towards the porch and Marina shrank even closer to Carlos. She felt his arm tightening round her; felt him too, slip his other hand into his pocket. Then, after what seemed to her an eternity she heard Jim's reply come snarling between his bruised lips:

"Naow—they'll have got further than this; they'll have made for the railway station by now."

He must have put his foot down on the accelerator as he spoke. The car shot forward and it felt to Marina as though her heart started to beat again.

She felt Carlos draw a deep breath and then his cheek was against hers and his lips against her hair whispering:

"We're lucky, my darling."

He moved away from her and touched the leather-covered door of the church. It moved and he said:

"It's open, come inside."

Marina followed him wonderingly.

The interior of the church, which was not a large one, was in darkness save for the flickering lights of the candles burning before the statues of saints and a great cluster of brightness in the Lady Chapel. There was a sweet tang of incense and a feeling, too, of peace. Marina thought it was as if she had stepped from the noise and tumult of a tempest into the calm serenity of a harbour.

"We've no time to waste," Carlos whispered at her side. "We'll change our clothes; it'll make us less conspicuous."

He took the bundle she had over her arm from

her as he spoke, and sorted out his suit and shirt
and gave her back her coat and skirt and blouse.

"Change quickly," he said. "There's no one here."

Without argument Marina moved to the very back
of the church behind the font. Slipping off her
brightly coloured skirt and blouse, she donned instead the blouse she had worn when they escaped
from Lisbon. It was badly in need of an iron, but
at least it was dry.

Because no woman is without her vanity even in
times of the most terrible danger, she could not help
hoping that her coat would hide its unkempt appear-
ance.

Somewhere in the darkness she could hear soft
movements that Carlos was making as he was changing. Then she buttoned her coat, feeling suddenly
cold.

She looked up and saw a little to the left of her
the sweet contemplative face of St Theresa of Lisieux.
It was a large statue and the roses in the Saint's
hand were vividly red, and the candles guttering
beneath it flickered in the almost imperceptible
draught and gave the impression that it was nothing
inanimate but something that lived and breathed.

"Help us to safety." The prayer came from Marina's heart and she added: "And help Carlos to love
me as I love him."

She almost felt as though she had spoken the
words aloud and then she knew that never in her
whole life had any prayer she had made meant so
much or been so much a part of her whole being.

On an impulse, without even wondering what Carlos would think, she knelt down at the Altar Rail.
She clasped her hands together and then she found he
was beside her, kneeling too, his head bent in prayer.

At that moment Marina felt that they were close

to one another and joined in a way they had never been before. It was as if the Saint above them blessed them, and blessed them together, as one person rather than two.

"He is mine and I am his," Marina thought simply, then once again she was praying with an intensity that was beyond thought and beyond words. She prayed with her body, her heart and her soul that their love would be blessed and a happy ending come to all they were going through.

"Please, God, help me!"

She felt as though her voice rang out and then knew it was a cry from within her and her lips had not moved.

She felt Carlos stir beside her. He raised his head and crossed himself and then he took her hand in his and kissed it and they rose together from their knees.

Carlos drew some money from his pocket and Marina heard the crackle of a crisp note as he slipped it into a box attached to the Altar Rails and she saw a little smile on his lips in the light from the candles.

"My favourite saint," he said. "I always pray to her when I'm in a predicament."

"And does she answer your prayer?" Marina asked, deeply serious.

"She has never failed me yet," he answered. "Come, darling, we can't linger here."

He turned to leave and Marina gave a little cry.

"I forgot your tie!" she said. "And Carlos, I never had time to iron your shirt."

"At least it's clean," he answered.

"No, wait a moment," Marina said. "I've an idea. Have you got a knife on you?"

He put his hand in a pocket and drew out something. She heard a slight click and then a wicked tongue of steel flashed in the candle-light.

"A flick knife!" Marina exclaimed. "Oh Carlos, how could you?"

"I might have needed it a few moments ago," he answered, "if I'd remembered I'd got it in my pocket when I entered the caravan, Jim Johnson would not be following us now."

"And the police would be wanting us for murder," Marina finished and added sharply: "Don't talk like that—I can't bear it."

She took the knife from him rather gingerly; then going to where she had left her coloured skirt, picked it up and hacked away at the hem.

Like most cheap garments the hem was bound with a different material. It was black and in a few moments Marina handed out to Carlos a long, dark, snakelike piece of rayon not unlike a tie.

"Put it round your neck," she said. "At least it looks more respectable than an open shirt."

He gave a little chuckle.

"We might be going to visit the duke!"

"Jim and his friends will be looking for a couple of colourful gypsies," Marina answered, looking to where Carlos's bright blue jeans and red and white shirt lay on the stone floor of the church.

She bent down as she spoke and picked up her own garments.

"Where are we going to put these?" she asked.

"Somewhere where they won't be found for some time," Carlos answered.

He picked up his own clothes and took hers from her. He rolled them into a ball and then with a sudden movement flung them as hard as he could high up over the doorway.

The inner doors of the church protruded forward and Marina saw vaguely there was a slight ledge edged with gold carving.

"Let's hope that no one finds them for at least twenty-four hours," Carlos said.

Marina gave a little smile.

"When they do, perhaps they will find a good use for them."

He took her hand in his.

"Come on—we've been here long enough."

He pulled open the leather covered door by which they had entered, stepped out of the peace and serenity of the church and it closed behind them with a soft sound not unlike a sigh.

Outside the street lamps were almost dazzling. Then Marina looked up at the sky, gave a little exclamation:

"The stars have gone!" she said. "It'll not be long before it's dawn."

Carlos did not seem particularly interested. Looking anxiously up and down the road outside and then taking Marina by the arm, he walked a little way to the left, then turned off the main street at the first side turning.

"Where're we going?" Marina asked.

"I don't know," Carlos answered. "I just want to be quite certain we don't meet your ex-boy friend."

The venom had gone from his tone, and Marina knew he was no longer angry, no longer jealous. Those moments in the church had brought him, she thought, the same solace as they had brought her.

There were rows of neat little surburban houses on each side of them. The curtains still drawn over every window, doors securely barred, the gateways to the gardens latched.

"We must find somebody soon," Marina said almost desperately.

As she spoke a car came swinging round the corner. It was a small, grey Peugeot, not unlike the one in which they had travelled from Paris. A young man got out outside a house a few yards ahead of them.

He was dressed in overalls, his face was dirty and he looked tired. He glanced in their direction and seemed intent on hurrying into the house, when Carlos spoke to him:

"Pardon, Monsieur," he said in French, "but I wonder if it would be possible for you to take us in your car to the airport? My wife and I had an accident with our own car and we have an aeroplane to catch."

"I regret, Monsieur," the young man answered, "but I am just going to bed. You will doubtless find someone else to accommodate you."

"I'm willing to pay most generously if you could help us," Carlos said.

As he spoke, he drew some notes from his pocket and added in almost conversational tone:

"Shall we say two hundred new francs?"

The young man stared in quite obvious astonishment.

"Monsieur," he expostulated; "that would be too much. The airport is only about fifteen minutes away."

"I'm still prepared to pay two hundred francs," Carlos repeated.

The young man glanced towards his front door as if almost unwilling to relinquish the idea of the comfort of his bed, then with a simple gesture he pointed to his car.

"It's not very comfortable, Monsieur, I'm afraid."

Before he had finished speaking, Carlos had opened the back door and helped Marina into the car. The young man got in front and started up the engine.

"You work at night?" Carlos asked politely.

"I'm on night shift at the factory," the driver answered. "Putting in a lot of overtime at the moment—exports for overseas."

"And that is good?" Carlos questioned.

"Good for some," the man answered, "but the hours are long and the pay should be better than it is."

He spoke surlily and Marina, anxious that they should not get into what could obviously be a political discussion, said hastily:

"The airport is a private one isn't it?"

The man nodded.

"Yes, and doing well, I believe. They've been operating for five years. There's talk of enlarging it and bringing in the State airways."

"You don't happen to know the name of the owners, do you?" Carlos asked.

"I can't say that I do. He's making a good thing out of it, if you ask me. When he first started, he only had one aeroplane—now he has twenty or more."

The driver spoke grudgingly as though he wasn't too pleased to hear of another man's success.

Carlos gave Marina's hand a little squeeze.

"Everything's going right," she thought. St Theresa had answered their prayers to let them get away to safety.

A few seconds later they turned into the gates of the aerodrome. There were a few huts, two big hangers and in the light of the dawn Marina could see two or three aeroplanes scattered around the edges of the landing ground.

"Here you are," the young man said, bringing the car to a standstill outside one of the huts.

He looked round with an expression that was half apprehensive and half aggressive as though he expected Carlos to argue now that the moment for payment had come.

Carlos merely handed him two one-hundred franc notes.

"*Merci, Monsieur*, You have been extremely kind," he said.

The young man took the notes as though he could hardly believe they were real; then finding his voice he said:

"*Merci, Monsieur. Au revoir* and *bon voyage.*"

He drove off before they had time to find out if the door of the hut was open. Carlos turned the handle: it was locked.

Without a word, they walked across the rough unfinished ground to the next hut. That was also locked.

"I wonder what time they come on duty?" Marina asked trying to keep the edge of disappointment out of her voice.

"There's sure to be a night watchman," Carlos said.

He walked towards the hangar, Marina following.

Sure enough, tucked away in the corner of the largest there was a small brazier burning brightly and an old man asleep with a sack over his knees for warmth and an ancient overcoat round his shoulders with the collar turned up to meet the dark beret which he had pulled low over his ears.

"*Bonjour, Monsieur!*" Carlos shouted at him and he woke with a start.

"What're you doing here?" he asked in a thick voice. "You're not allowed in this hangar."

"I want to know what time your boss comes on duty," Carlos answered. "We wish to charter an aeroplane."

"Clients, are you?"

The old man pulled his beret high on his head so that his ears were free and it was easier to hear. He peered at them as though to satisfy himself that they were the type of client who could pay for a chartered 'plane and got slowly to his feet.

"I'll let you into the waiting-room," he said. "The first flight this morning is for six o'clock. Someone should be along soon."

He appeared to be talking to himself rather than to them.

Carlos said sharply:

"Where's the six o'clock 'plane going?"

"No idea," the man answered. "They don't tell me what they're up to. I goes home as soon as they come to work."

He disentangled his legs from the sack, laid it down on the packing case on which he had been sitting, and very slowly led the way from the hangar back towards the huts.

He had difficulty in inserting the key in the lock, but finally the door was open and he ushered them inside.

"You can wait here," he said. "They shouldn't be long now."

The waiting-room was chill and not particularly inviting. There were a few chairs scattered around small tables and a profusion of ancient magazines. The bar which stood at one end was closed and somewhat ostentatiously padlocked.

"Thank you very much," Carlos said.

He slipped a few francs into the old man's hand, who seemed astonished but pocketed them quickly.

"*Merci, Monsieur—merci beaucoup*," he muttered as he shuffled away.

"What's the time?" Marina asked when they were alone.

Carlos looked at his watch.

"I'm not quite certain," he said. "My watch seems

233

to have stopped. Perhaps it got a bang when I hit Jim Johnson. Anyway if, as the old man says, the first aeroplane is going off at six o'clock, it oughtn't to be long.

When they had been shown into the waiting-room, the old man had switched on the light. Marina looked at Carlos now for the first time and gave a little chuckle.

"You really look surprisingly neat for all you have gone through," she said, "and your tie was an inspiration."

"I'll go and look at myself in the glass," Carlos answered.

"I'll do the same," Marina agreed.

"Wait a minute."

He put out his hand and stopped her as she turned towards the cloakroom at the far end of the waiting-room.

"I've got something to tell you."

"What is it?" she asked apprehensively.

"Only that you're lovely," he answered. "I've seen you in so many different ways now—dressed to the nines the night we went out in Lisbon—how long ago that seems—tousled and sleepy when we had to sit up all night in the train; flamboyant and very provocative dressed as a girl from the circus and now—" he stopped.

"Yes, now?" Marina prompted.

"Adorable."

"You're flattering me," Marina said a little unsteadily. "I'm quite certain I look awful. Thank goodness my makeup's in that case. I won't run anywhere without taking that with me."

She had spoken laughingly, but any further conversation was impossible. Carlos's arm went round her and Carlos's lips were seeking hers. He kissed her passionately, it seemed to her with a difference.

She was not certain what it was, but the ecstasy he had always evoked in her made her whole body tingle and she thought she would always remember this dingy little waiting-room with the naked electric light bulb high above their heads.

"Darling, you're quite wonderful," Carlos whispered. "You've never failed me—not even in the tightest corners."

"They haven't mattered," Marina said. "We've been together through them all, haven't we?"

"Yes, together," he answered.

She sensed rather than heard the note of finality in his tone. "He is going to leave me," she thought frantically. "This is the end, the last journey; and when we get back to Lisbon, he'll go away and I'll never see him again."

Because the thought was like a wound in her heart she flung her arms round his neck:

"Darling, darling Carlos," she whispered. "Everything has been worth it. The fear, the discomfort—everything."

She felt his arms tighten around her, then the door opened behind them and they sprang apart almost guiltily.

A short, thick-set man with a small cigar at the corner of his mouth came into the room. He seemed as startled to see them as they had been at his interruption.

"I didn't know anyone was here," he said and added quickly: "Do you want something or are you just trespassing?"

Carlos seemed quite unruffled.

"Are you the proprietor?" he enquired. "We were

235

waiting for you to arrive as we wish to charter an aeroplane."

"I think we could accommodate you," the Frenchman replied crisply.

He took a key from his pocket as he spoke and opened a door which was marked "Office", at the end of the room. The door swung open.

"Where do you want to go?" the proprietor asked casually and over his shoulder as though he wasn't interested.

Carlos followed him slowly with a dignity that was somehow impressive into a small office. It was an untidy room with a desk stacked with papers in the middle of it; with maps—some hanging crookedly —lining the walls.

"I wish to go to Lisbon," Carlos said.

The proprietor, who had seated himself at the desk, looked up, surprise in his eyes.

"How strange!" he remarked.

"Strange?" Carlos queried.

"Yes," the proprietor answered, his eyes narrowing. "Two men came here yesterday and made enquiries as to whether I had been asked to carry any passengers to Lisbon or Geneva. I told them the truth. I had not taken a 'plane to either place in the last ten years at least."

"Well, I wish to go to Lisbon," Carlos said. "And I'm prepared to pay not only the fare, but for the flight to be entirely and completely secret."

The Frenchman looked up at him speculatively.

"Are the police involved in this?"

Carlos shook his head.

"I promise you there's nothing like that," he said.

"Then why the enquiries?"

The man's attitude was hostile and Marina thought

with despair that any moment the interview might end in a row and disaster; but to her surprise Carlos smiled a charming, ingratiating smile.

"We will be truthful," he said quietly. "And of course we must rely on your discretion. My wife and I have eloped."

For a moment the proprietor stared at him and then his face creased into an answering smile.

"A love affair!"

He slapped his hand on his thigh in appreciation.

"Exactly, Monsieur—a love affair," Carlos repeated. "My wife and I were married only yesterday. She is a rich woman, or she will be when her father dies. He wishes that his money should be in the hands of someone of his own choosing. You're a man of the world, Monsieur. You will understand all too well the things that have been said about me."

"And they're not true?"

"Even if they were it would not matter. We're in love."

The Frenchman let out a great guffaw of laughter, then he looked at Marina and his eyes twinkled.

"I do not blame you, Monsieur, Madame is enchanting," he said.

"Allow me to present her," Carlos said.

It was a formality that would not have been out of place at a diplomat's party.

"Madame Ayola, my wife: and you, Monsieur? I'm afraid I do not know your name."

"Boussac," the Frenchman said, "at your service, Madame."

He raised Marina's fingers to his lips with almost a courtly grace and then briskly, the cordiality finished, he sat down at his desk.

"An aeroplane, Monsieur," he said. "to Lisbon is

going to cost you a lot of money. My discretion, of course, need not be rewarded, but you will understand, there is the pilot to be considered."

"Of course, of course," Carlos said.

"These things are not easy," the Frenchman continued: "there are difficulties—passports—yours are in order, I suppose?"

"But of course," Carlos replied, "except that Madame's remains in her maiden name. We have not yet had time to get it changed."

"That will not matter, Monsieur," Boussac said. "Now, let me see—"

He started to scribble an incredible number of figures down on his blotting paper. Finally he announced:

"I think the sum will be three thousand, nine hundred New Francs, Monsieur."

Marina gave a little gasp, but Carlos seemed quite unperturbed.

"You will not, I hope, mind taking travellers' cheques?" he enquired.

"No, of course not," the Frenchman agreed. Carlos looked at Marina and held out his hand.

"I'm sorry this should be necessary," he said.

It was the first time he had not been able to pay for everything and just for a moment the old bogey which had always haunted her, of men who were after her money, reared its ugly head. Then as quickly as it had been there, it was gone and impulsively Marina handed him her handbag.

"There are £250 in travellers' cheques," she said, "and quite a number of pound notes; I'm not sure how many."

Carlos drew some notes from his pocket, counted them and set them down in front of Monsieur Boussac.

"My wife's cheques are in sterling," he said. "Do you know the exchange?"

Monsieur Boussac drew a card from a folder on his desk.

"Here are the prices I was prepared to give yesterday," he said. "You will, I think, not quarrel over the fact they are a few cents less than you can obtain in the town."

"We're in agreement over everything," said Carlos suavely.

Marina signed half her cheques and handed them to Carlos who handed them to Boussac. He stacked them with Carlos's notes in a neat pile on his blotter, then he picked up the telephone.

It was a long and what appeared to be a heated conversation over which aeroplane should be used, who should navigate and what time it could be ready. It seemed to Marina as though every possible obstacle was being put in the way of their leaving; and then, as Monsieur Boussac put down the telephone, he said with what appeared almost an angelic smile:

"The 'plane should be ready in twenty minutes. I dare say, while Monsieur and Madame are waiting, they would like to celebrate? We have in the bar a quite good selection of champagne."

Carlos paid for the champagne, most of which was consumed by Monsieur Boussac, but Marina was more interested in discovering if they could buy some packets of biscuits and tins of foie gras which they could take with them on the aeroplane.

"Had there been time, I could perhaps have arranged for some coffee to be brought in from a nearby café," Monsieur Boussac said as he finished off the champagne.

There was no regret in his tone and Marina wondered if they had been firmer whether coffee could have been provided without the expense of the champagne. But she was not prepared to quibble or even question anything Monsieur Boussac did.

All she was longing for was the moment when they could get in the aeroplane and leave. She had an uncomfortable feeling that Carlos was as anxious as she was, even though he did not show it.

More than once she caught him glancing out of the window, but he made no other show of impatience.

When finally, escorted by Monsieur Boussac, they walked from the hut towards the waiting 'plane he did not appear to hurry.

Only as they reached the top of the gangway and stood for a moment to say their last farewells, did Marina glance at the road along which they had come and see approaching the gateway of the aerodrome a large grey car.

She had never seen the car before. It evoked no memories and yet at the same time it gave her a feeling of uneasiness.

She waved to Monsieur Boussac and hurriedly bending her head went through the door of the aeroplane and through into the cabin.

The door was shut, the engines already started up and now they were taxi-ing slowly down the runway.

Marina looked through the porthole. She could see from the angle at which they were moving that the grey car had drawn up outside the hut. Two men were getting out.

She only had a glimpse of them, but somehow they seemed not unlike the two men who had come to her bedroom that night in Lisbon.

Perhaps she was mistaken. Perhaps everywhere

she saw enemies—a greater danger than Jim Johnson and his bullies had ever constituted.

She shivered and her hands went out to Carlos who was sitting beside her.

"It's all right," he said soothingly. "I have a feeling Boussac will keep his word."

There was no need for explanation, no need to tell Carlos what she thought and what she had felt. He had taken up the conversation once again almost at the point her thoughts had reached.

"Do you think he really will?" she asked.

"I should say he's a difficult man—but in his own way an honourable man. He has taken our money, and he has given us his word of honour. I don't believe he'll break it."

"Supposing they offer him more than we've given him?"

"I doubt it," Carlos said. "They are much more likely to try and bully him and Boussac is not the sort of man to be bullied."

"No, I think you're right," Marina said.

She had not liked the Frenchman, yet now she could see there was a kind of integrity about him and the inevitable soft spot where a pair of lovers was concerned. She gave a little sigh almost of relief.

"How vulnerable the French are when it comes to affairs of the heart," she said.

"How vulnerable we all are," Carlos answered.

She put her head against his shoulder, content for the moment to lean against him, to know the comfort of his presence.

The sound of the engine was mesmeric. The pilot was sitting ahead of them, his ears covered unable to hear anything they said.

They were almost alone above the world.

Already the small plane was diving into the clouds; and now they were above them in the sunshine, the land of nowhere, where nothing mattered except themselves.

"What are we going to do when we get to Lisbon," Marina asked almost dreamily, thinking where they might stay, where they could go where no one would find them.

"That depends on if I can find Pedro. I'm sure there'll be a message for me," Carlos said.

Marina sat up stiffly and stared:

"You mean you might have to leave at once?" she asked. "You might have to go back to Culuna?"

"You know that's got to happen," Carlos said.

"Has it?" Marina asked.

It was a cry of fear. He did not seem to have heard it.

"If not, I'm a man without a country, a man without a purpose," he said bitterly.

She saw the expression on his face and realised that he had forgotten her. Once again the barrier had come between them; the barrier which, she thought sadly, always resulted in her being on the outside.

12

The pilot turned his head.

"I shall be landing in a few minutes, Monsieur," he said. "Will you and Madame fasten your seat belts."

Carlos leant across Marina helping her to fasten hers. She felt the touch of his hand; almost without seeing his face so close to hers she wondered if anyone would ever again bring her that same feeling of ecstatic excitement and the kind of trembling joy which she could not explain and yet which rippled through her like the movement of a stream over cool rocks.

With an effort, because she felt that if she said anything affectionate or loving she would burst into tears, she asked:

"What are we going to do when we arrive?"

Carlos sat back in his own seat.

"I've been trying to make plans," he said. "So much hinges on whether Pedro is there waiting for us."

"Why should he be?" Marina asked in surprise. "He couldn't know we're coming."

"We made an arrangement," Carlos replied, "that if the project was hopeless Pedro would return to Lisbon in a week's time."

"You didn't tell me this," Marina said almost accusingly.

"I tried not to think about it," Carlos answered.

"I tried not to acknowledge even to myself that we might fail."

"Poor Carlos," Marina murmured beneath her breath.

She put out her hand as though to touch his, then changed her mind.

"And if Pedro isn't waiting for us, which somehow seems to be unlikely, what do we do then?" she asked.

"I think we will go to a small, unobtrusive hotel somewhere along the coast," Carlos answered. "Not Estoril of course. Somewhere where we might be lost amongst the holiday makers."

"The first thing we had better do then, is to buy ourselves some luggage," Marina said. "I am told the hotels are invariably suspicious of people who arrive without a suitcase of any sort, especially if they look like us."

There was a hint of laughter in her voice as she glanced at Carlos's creased shirt and home-made tie.

He turned to look at her and the smile softened the severity of his expression.

"To me you appear lovely," he said. "You always do."

She wanted to believe him, wanted to hear more, but the question that was bursting inside her forged its way through her lips:

"And after that?" she asked. "After we have hidden ourselves amongst the tourists, and you have managed to contact Pedro, what then?"

He looked away from her and his profile was stern and uncompromising.

"You know the answer to that question," he said.

She knew she should not have asked, but her whole being cried out in revolt against tamely accepting

244

the inevitability of their parting. She wanted to plead with him. She wanted to ask him if these days and nights of danger together had meant nothing. She wanted to know whether their kisses, so passionate, so compelling, so utterly wonderful, had been just an amusement where he was concerned.

Though her pride prevented her doing any of these things she felt the tears prick her eyelids and feeling of suffocation in her throat.

"We're going down."

It was the pilot who spoke.

Instinctively Marina ceased to look at Carlos and turned her face towards the window on her left. She could see the aerodrome below them. She could see the fields and woods tinged with the green of spring; the silver of the river winding its way to the sea.

The aeroplane swung a little and now she could only see the sea reflecting the blue sky and stretching away into the misty horizon. It was over this sea that Carlos would fly away from her, disappearing towards the west from which she knew, in her heart, he would never return.

She found herself wondering what platitudes they would say in farewell. "Thank you for a lovely time?" How could they say that?

Yet, despite all the danger, the discomfort, the fear, the terror, for her anyway, it had been the loveliest and happiest time she had ever known in her whole life.

She thought of London, of New York, of Paris—of everywhere else she would go; the endless parties, the chatter of her so-called friends; the pattern of travelling from place to place, of going from one comfortable residence to another, whether it was hotel, apartment or a friend's house—there was little to choose between any of them. It all seemed unreal, utterly and absolutely pointless.

"We're going to land," Carlos said and put his hand over hers as if to reassure her.

She felt the strength of his fingers and because she could not control her reaction to his touch she clasped her own hand tightly about his, feeling a kind of desperate comfort because their palms were close against each other.

Vaguely, at the back of her mind, she hoped he would think she was frightened of landing. Somehow it no longer mattered what he thought. She only knew the sands were running out; they only had a little more time together.

The wheels of the aeroplane touched the ground with hardly a jolt. They taxied along over the tarmac and finally came to rest a little way from the main building.

Carlos thanked the pilot. They all shook hands; then a gangway was brought to the door of the 'plane and Marina stepped out into the sunshine.

She remembered the last time she had landed at Lisbon Airport. It seemed months, almost years, ago and yet it had only been a few days. She had been running away from Victor.

Now she asked nothing more than to be able to go on running not only from Victor but from the sinister people called "they", from Jim Johnson, anyone, so long as Carlos could be beside her.

They walked slowly towards the entrance to the Airport. An official ushered them fussily through the Customs. They were asked if they had any luggage and when Carlos said "None" it was indicated that they could go through to the Entrance Hall.

It was not very large and there were a number of people hurrying backwards and forwards, staring at the indicator, buying newspapers, asking innumerable questions of harassed officials.

Carlos stood staring about him. Marina closed her eyes.

"Oh God, don't let him find Pedro. Don't let him be here," she prayed, and knew that her prayer was refused for Carlos gave a sudden cry.

"There he is!" he exclaimed and leaving her side he ran towards the bookstall.

A small dark, middle-aged man stood with his back to them, turning over the magazines.

"Pedro!"

Marina could hear Carlos's voice. She saw the other man turn eagerly and their hands meet.

She stood where Carlos had left her alone and indecisive. The thought came to her that if this were a film or a television play she would walk away now while they were still engaged in talking and save all the embarrassment of goodbyes and all the heartache of the last desperate, inadequate words of explanations and farewell.

But, although she knew it would be the right and brave thing to do, she couldn't do it. She couldn't leave him. She must stay to the bitter end. Finish the dream and see the despair and despondency on his face and know she could do nothing about it.

Perhaps it was almost worse than anything else, she thought, to know she must stand by and see him suffer. She could not help him.

"I love him more than I thought," she told herself with a wistful twist of her lips.

She knew in that moment that if she could give Carlos what he wanted, she would give it to him even though she would have no participation in it and it would merely mean they would have to say "Good-

247

bye" even more quickly than if he had nowhere to go and nothing to do.

"He doesn't want me," she whispered and tried to stiffen her pride with words which she knew were meaningless.

She would wait; she would stand by and listen for the last expression of his love before they parted for ever.

She could see Carlos with his back to her, see Pedro talking to him animatedly gesticulating, and instinctively she opened her bag to find her vanity case and powder her nose.

As she did so she saw her book of travellers' cheques, depleted now because of the number of cheques she had signed away. But there was some money left and she wondered how she could force Carlos to take them without hurting his pride.

"I'll pay you back," he had said as she signed away her pounds to Monsieur Boussac. It had been a statement of fact. How easy to reply, "Don't worry—it means nothing to me."

But already she knew Carlos well enough to know that he would not accept her money and that however poor he might be in the future she would be repaid. "How can I help him? What can I do?"

She knew as she stared at her face in the tiny mirror of her gold vanity box that she had never felt so helpless, so inconsequential. She could neither keep the man she loved at her side, nor assist him. All her wealth, all her influence, all the things which seemed so much a part and parcel of her life were useless.

Angrily, because she could hardly bear to look at herself, she snapped her vanity case shut and put it in her bag. As she did so, she heard a voice ejaculate her name:

"Marina!"

She turned her head. Standing only a few yards away from her was Victor.

She seemed to take in everything about him at one glance. His exquisitely cut grey Savile Row suit, his Brigade tie, his polished shoes from Lobb, his Cartier watch, and behind him she could see a great pile of luggage being pushed on a trolley by a porter, luggage which she recognized because it was so familiar, red and white stripes of a particular pattern which she had made exclusively her own.

"Marina, what're you doing here? What the hell's all this about? We've been nearly off our heads worrying about you."

"Worrying about me? Why?"

"Don't be so ridiculous!" Victor spoke almost sharply. "Sybil tried to get hold of you the day after you had left. Your Trustees wanted you to sign some papers—something rather important, I gather. Anyway, we rang every hotel in Lisbon only to learn you had disappeared."

"They told her that?" Marina asked.

"Of course they told her," Victor answered. "They said you had not booked out and all your clothes were left behind. Sybil was frantic I can tell you; in fact so frantic she told me the whole story. What have you been up to, Marina? What have you done to yourself?"

His eyes travelled over her. There was a look of near stupefaction. Marina knew what he was seeing; the untidy, un-set hair; the creased, un-ironed blouse; the suit which was showing such obvious signs of wear and tear; the low-heeled sandals which had been meant to go with her cotton skirt.

"What's happened? If I hadn't found you I was just about to go to the police."

"You haven't done that?" Marina asked quickly.

"That's what I've come over for," Victor said. "We couldn't understand why you should go away without taking your clothes. Anyway, I've brought you some more."

Marina looked at the great pile of red and white suitcases.

"I suppose I ought to say thank you," she said slowly.

"Look here, Marina, this isn't good enough," Victor answered. "You've got Sybil into hysterics and I've been pretty anxious myself, I can tell you. You can't do this sort of thing, you know."

"I don't think I shall ever do it again, anyway," Marina said almost beneath her breath.

She looked to where Carlos and Pedro were still talking and then, in a voice that seemed to come from the very depths of despair she said:

"It's all right, Victor. I'm ready to come home now."

"Let's be thankful for that," Victor replied.

He spoke testily, and Marina realised he had been shaken out of his habitual calm. Somehow it didn't matter.

"Well, come along," he said. "I except there is a car to meet me."

He put out his hand as if to take her arm.

Now Carlos was coming towards them and Marina stood watching him, her whole heart in her eyes. She expected him to look despondent. Instead he was smiling.

"Darling!" he said when he was within earshot. "It's good news—wonderful news."

"What's happened?" Marina enquired.

"It's over! The revolt is over!" Carlos answered, a note of excitement in his voice she had never heard before. "The communist leader has gone into hiding and most of his men have been killed. I told you the people loved my father. They have avenged him."

"I'm glad, terribly glad," Marina said.

Somewhere in the distance she heard Victor ask testily:

"Who's this, Marina?"

She didn't even turn her head. Carlos was holding both her hands in his.

"They want me back," he said. "I've already been elected President in my absence. Oh God, I can't begin to tell you what this means to me!"

"I'm glad, so glad for you," Marina said.

She could feel emotion vibrating from him and his fingers held hers so tightly that they hurt.

"What is going on?" Victor asked in a voice of thunder, and this time both Carlos and Marina turned to look at him.

"Who's this?" Carlos asked, repeating the same question that Victor had asked earlier.

"This is Victor Harrison," Marina answered, "a friend of mine."

"Friend be damned!" Victor ejaculated. "I would like you to know, sir, whoever you may be, that Miss Martyn is in my charge. I have come here from England to collect her and I intend taking her back with me right away."

"Miss Martyn?"

Carlos raised his eyebrows. The name was a question.

"I haven't had time to tell you," Marina began, but Victor interrupted her.

"Yes, Marina Martyn," he almost shouted, "and don't tell me that name is a surprise to you, because whatever you've been up to I'm perfectly certain that her very stupid and amateurish disguise, which

I would not have permitted had I known about it, was penetrated by you at the very first moment of your acquaintance."

Marina gave a little gasp. She continued to hold onto Carlos's hands. She felt as though she dared not let him go; that if she released her hold on him he would slip away and she would never be able to tell him.

It wasn't because she didn't trust him that she hadn't revealed her secret, simply because it hadn't seemed important. They loved each other and it didn't matter who either of them was.

"Please, Carlos," she said in a low voice, almost as though she hoped Victor wouldn't hear her. "Please, Carlos, listen to me."

"I don't know what all this is about," Carlos said in a bewildered manner. "Marina, I've got to talk to you. Pedro says there's an aeroplane this afternoon."

"Oh, Carlos, so soon?"

"I must get back," he said simply. "Surely you understand that?"

"Will you please attend to me," Victor thundered. "I want to know what's been going on here."

"Oh, Victor, do be quiet," Marina said as though one might talk to a refractory child.

"I will not," he replied. "I'm responsible for you, Marina. You know as well as I do that you didn't mean those ridiculous things you said the last time we were together. You've got to have someone to look after you, to care for you; you can't go rushing about the world, disappearing in this crazy fashion and upsetting everyone: besides, God knows what might have happened to you."

Carlos slowly disengaged his hands from Marina's.

"I don't know what all this is about," he said. "Is this man anything to you?"

He asked the question directly of Marina and she answered him without a moment's hesitation.

"Nothing, He means nothing, Carlos. He's trying to be kind. When they found out I had left the hotel without any luggage they became anxious."

"Oh, I see. That does take a bit of explaining."

"You see," Marina went on. "I ought to have told you ages ago that I was Marina Martyn. Somehow it didn't seem important."

"It wasn't important," Carlos said: "or should it have been?"

She saw in his face, the expression of his eyes, something she had never believed possible and never dreamed would happen. One man at least in the whole world didn't know who Marina Martyn was—Marina Marshall, Marina Martyn—they were both the same.

She knew him so well by now, every inflexion of his voice, every expression on his face, and had he been pretending to be ignorant she would have known it.

"Now don't let's have any nonsense," Victor said pompously. "You know who Marina Martyn is and, as I've already said, I'm quite certain you've known this ill-disguised secret from the very start."

"I'm sorry," Carlos said, addressing himself to Victor for the first time, "but I honestly don't know what you're talking about. Who is this Marina Martyn? A film star? I'm afraid I'm very, very ignorant of European personalities."

Marina gave a little gurgle of laughter and linked her arm through his.

"Oh, Carlos," she said, "you're shaking the very foundations of Victor's world. He doesn't understand."

"Is it important?" Carlos asked seriously.

Marina shook her head.

"Not in the least," she answered.

"Let's talk about what is important," he said. "We leave at three o'clock."

"We?"

She pulled back from him staring up at him, the colour draining away from her face leaving her deadly pale.

"Of course," he answered. "You know I wouldn't go without you now, not when it's safe—or at least comparatively."

"Safe?" Marina repeated. "That's not the point. I thought . . ."

He clasped his hand over hers and said:

"I know what you thought, darling. I couldn't help it. How could I ask you to go back and face certain death or stay here in absolute penury. I had nothing to offer you either way until now."

"Don't you understand?" Marina said. "I . . ."

She was going to say. "I would have gone with you barefoot to the end of the world," but he prevented her.

"I know," he said, "and I loved you for it, and some day I'll make up to you for all you have been through, for all you have suffered on my account. Now the only thing that matters is, we can go home, you and I together. We will be married as soon as we arrive. My people will love it. A wedding is almost as good as a coronation."

There was a smile of happiness on his lips and his eyes were shining. It was typical of him, Marina thought. He didn't ask her if she was willing to go. He didn't even ask her if she would marry him. He just knew their love was past all those unnecessary questions.

He wanted her and she wanted him, and now that his own particular code of honour was satisfied, he would take her masterfully and commandingly as he had carried her with him these last few days of their mad, impetuous escape from his enemies.

"Oh, Carlos!"

There was nothing else Marina could say. She felt as though the airport whirled around her. Somehow the black cloud of despair which had enveloped her all during their flight from France, had been swept away by one magical flick of Carlos's finger, and now sunlight was pouring over them both, golden, radiant and so dazzling that her eyes were blinded by it.

Somewhere, far away in the world which didn't belong to them she could hear Victor puffing and expostulating.

"I don't know what all this is about. Who's this fellow, Marina? How can you marry him? Who is he?"

His voice seemed to be part of the bustle and commotion of the Airport and then a little pang of pity for Victor, because he would never know the happiness that suffused her, never know the wonder that was hardly of this world, made Marina say gently:

"I am sorry, Victor. It's too long a story to have to explain it now. Thank you for bringing my clothes. I shall need them because I'm going to Culuna this afternoon."

"You can't. It's impossible! Culuna! Why, that's in South America."

"Yes, I know," Marina answered.

She turned back to Carlos.

"I expect you want to talk to Pedro," she said gently, anticipating his need as a wife should always anticipate the needs of her husband. "And I want to meet him too."

"Come along then," Carlos said. "Actually, there's so much to hear. Pedro got through on the telephone this morning. It's incredible what has happened."

Impetuously he turned towards his countryman who was waiting tactfully where he had left him by the bookstall.

Marina turned back for one moment.

"Good-bye, Victor," she said to a bewildered man who somehow looked smaller and less important than he had a few seconds earlier. "Good-bye, and thank you for coming. I'll write to you. I'll write to Sybil, too. Don't worry about me."

"But Marina, this is impossible—" Victor began, but already she had gone running with Carlos towards the bookstall, hand in hand like two excited children.

But before they could reach Pedro, the porter with the luggage blocked their path and Carlos looked down at Marina.

"He loves you, that man," he said. "Why don't you marry him?"

It was his old trick of knowing what was going on without being told and Marina smiled back at him happily.

"I don't love him," she said simply.

"Do you love me?"

The question was fierce, demanding, possessive.

"I love you, Carlos—I love you so much."

Just for a moment their eyes met. In the split second of time it seemed as though everything—even Culuna—faded into insignificance, except themselves.

"I love you," Carlos said softly.

It was almost a vow; and then eagerly, their faces alight, he turned to where Pedro was waiting to tell them the plans for their journey home.